PRAISE FOR

"His clever dialogue will leave readers in stitches.
— *Publishers Weekly*

"Known for his quirky, entertaining mysteries, Chris
Well does it again." — *RT Book Reviews*

"It is so easy to become involved in Chris Well's
books. The characters are real and the action is fast."
— *Armchair Interviews*

"Well serves up brisk dialogue."
— *Booklist* (American Library Association)

Cover design by Allie Krukowski

TOO GOOD TO BE TRUMAN

CHRIS WELL

TOO GOOD TO BE TRUMAN

For Erica

ONE

The man answered on the first ring. "This is Jack Carlin."

Harry Truman pinched his nose to disguise his voice. "Hello, is this the crime reporter who replaced that awful Harry Truman?"

"Why, yes it is. Are you a fan of my column?"

"I have a hot tip for you—I would not trust anyone else with this."

"Yeah?" You could almost hear Carlin salivating. "What is it?"

"There's going to be a drug deal tonight at Percy Priest Lake. And I happen to know that the buyer is a major player in Nashville city government. I thought you might want to be there to take pictures and get the big scoop."

"Have you told the cops?"

"Of course not—the police would show up and scare the guys off. If you want to expose this festering corruption, you need to be out there alone."

"I see what you mean. Can you tell me when this drug deal is taking place?"

"Sometime between ten o'clock tonight and six o'clock tomorrow morning."

"Can't you be more specific?"

"The council member—I'm sorry, I mean, the 'buyer'—is very nervous about this deal, and wants to be absolutely certain nobody else is around when the deal takes place. You see, this is a black market drug of a, well, shall we say, a personal nature."

"You mean—"

"I'd rather not say on an unprotected line. But you just need to make sure that you are hidden good and tight. If they see anyone else out there, the whole thing will fall through. But I know you can do this. You need to show all those people who say you're not fit to write on Harry Truman's toilet paper."

"They say that?"

"If you get this scoop tonight, they won't be saying it anymore."

"I didn't know they were saying that."

"Trust me, they're saying it. But I believe in you, Jack Carlin."

Truman hung up the phone. If he knew Carlin, the man would spend all night hiding in the weeds and the mud waiting for a transaction that would never happen.

His good deed done for the day, Truman got back to work. Sitting at his kitchen table, he stared at the words on the screen. This was his first novel. This was the first page of his first novel. This was the first sentence of his first novel.

In fact, in the four months since he had embarked on his new career as a novelist, this was the sum total of his oeuvre: "The night was dark."

He had spent days staring at that sentence. He had spent sleepless nights mulling it over and over in his mind. Imagining how he could reshape it. How he could enhance it. How he could expand upon it.

For a period of time he'd toyed with adding that the night was also "stormy." He had successfully talked himself out of it.

And now he stared. As he had stared nearly every day for the past one hundred twenty days. Give or take.

In the span of his career as a novelist (all four months of it), he had gone through some changes—

from a man who would rise bright and early, eat a hearty breakfast, and gladly face the challenges of the new day; to a man who started having bourbon with his breakfast; to a man who had bourbon for breakfast.

He picked up his glass and looked at it. He was almost out of breakfast. Truman went to the living room to lie on the worn couch, rest his eyes, and wait for the muse to come visit him. He thought of the muses as they were portrayed in the 1980s movie musical *Xanadu*. Olivia Newton John's portrayal indicated that the muses weren't in any kind of hurry. After all, she waited, what, forty years to finally do anything about Gene Kelly's dream. And she didn't do squat for the other guy. What was that actor's name?

Truman would have jumped on the Information Superhighway to look it up, but he didn't really care. Not to mention, his Internet had recently been cut off.

As a former newspaper writer — a crime reporter for a major metropolitan newspaper — Truman knew the secret to writing was not waiting for the muse. The secret was to sit down and write. Rain or shine, inspiration or no inspiration, hell or high water.

But you also needed to care. And he had a hard time caring about this book.

He was relieved to hear the local postal carrier out in the hall, the wheels on the man's cart squeaking as they rolled by his door. The jangle of keys. The opening of the big metal door to the rows of mailboxes for this building.

Once the sound of the ritual had finished, and the squeaking cart disappeared back down the hall,

Truman dragged himself off the couch and ambled across the apartment to the door. Past the beat-up folding card table, which served as a poker table every Wednesday night, and doubled as a dinner table on the rare occasions when he entertained; past the old television set which, without cable, got all of three channels; a collection of second-hand Reader's Digest hardcovers, which held abbreviated editions of what must originally have been some unnecessarily wordy books; and a big chair that looked more comfortable than it was.

Truman cracked the door and peeked before actually exiting his apartment. Most of the neighbors on this floor were busybodies; old biddies that'd outlasted their men, who now placed all their worldly affection on tiny, angry dogs that invariably thought of Truman's shoes as fire hydrants.

Determining it was safe to venture out, he leaped across the hall and jammed his key in the mailbox for apartment 356. He grabbed his mail, snapped the door shut, and locked it.

"Oh, Mr. Trumbull!"

That would be Mrs. Gill, the middle-aged divorcee who had misheard his name during introductions. He'd never told her the difference, and now it was just awkward. He made for his apartment like he didn't hear her calling his name—or, rather, didn't hear her calling the name that she called him.

She intercepted him at the door. "Mr. Trumbull, how are you this afternoon?"

Afternoon? Of course. After all, he had just gotten his mail. He'd wasted half the day waiting for the stupid muse to swing by. Or, for that matter, a visit from the Will to Live.

He forced a smile. "I'm doing about the usual."

"I was going to make chili tonight. I thought maybe you'd like to come over for dinner and have some."

"As much as I'd love to, I really need to keep hammering on this book. I'm really beginning to make progress. Thanks, anyway." He showed teeth, hoping it looked friendly. He squeaked through the door and shut it behind him. He really wished she'd just get a dog and be done with it. At least with the dogs, he knew where he stood.

When it came to women, Truman was through with that noise. If the first divorce didn't get the message through to his thick head, the second divorce certainly did. And that third divorce just confirmed his suspicions. He was in no hurry to take auditions for ex-wife number four.

He threw the mail on the poker table and went to the cabinet for another shot of breakfast. Of course, now that he realized it was the afternoon, it was time to think about moving on to the hard stuff.

Back at the table with liquid nourishment in hand, Truman started to sift through the mail. Bill. (Second notice.) Bill. (Final notice.) Letter from his ex-wife. (The third one.) Letter from her lawyer.

Here was a renewal notice from the newspaper that fired him. He folded the envelope into a lopsided paper airplane and aimed it for the wastebasket by the TV. It almost made it.

He didn't need no stinkin' subscription. Granted, he picked up the newspaper every Tuesday without fail. He would turn right to Jack Carlin's crime column, clip it out, and throw out the rest of the newspaper unread. Then, felt tip marker in hand,

Truman would write up a comprehensive list of corrections. (Sometimes he'd even go out on his own dime and re-investigate some of Carlin's reporting, just to find out what actually happened.) Once his assessment was complete, Truman mailed the marked-up column, along with any appendixes, to his former editor, Francis Withers.

He'd done this every week for four months. And that idiot Carlin was still working there.

Once upon a time, a good reporter was prized by a newspaper. But when the owner of this paper, Leopold Miller, got tired of his ace crime reporter digging up the truth, he sent down the word from on high to cut loose Harry Truman. There was brief talk of suggesting Truman take a "sabbatical," but seeing as how these days newspapers were already wheezing their last breath before the meteor hit, management decided it would be more efficient to just cut him loose and be done with it. And once you've been cut loose, you suddenly find yourself unwelcome at every media news outlet known to man.

The next envelope was from a local charity. He folded this envelope, too, and threw it in the general direction of the wastebasket. The clumpy paper airplane didn't fare any better than its predecessor.

The next envelope bore the logo of his book publisher. Fortunately, the contracts for this book deal were too far down the line to cancel before anyone of consequence in New York heard what happened. Which meant he got his severance check on a Friday, and his book advance on a Monday. Truman had cashed the check pronto, before anyone in New York could think better of it.

So, when the members of the publishing committee changed their minds, all they could do was ask for their money back. Which they had been doing for the past several weeks. Opening this envelope from the publisher now, he was greeted with the most sternly worded please-send-back-the-check letter yet.

Truman went to the laptop and typed up the warmest reply he could think of.

SIRS,
I WAS PLEASED TO RECEIVE YOUR RECENT LETTER. YOUR KIND WISHES AND YOUR MORAL SUPPORT MEAN MORE TO ME THAN YOU COULD EVER KNOW. PLEASE KNOW THAT I AM STILL WORKING NIGHT AND DAY ON THIS BOOK. BY THE WAY, IF YOU HAVE ATTEMPTED TO CONTACT ME VIA EMAIL, PLEASE NOTE THAT I AM CURRENTLY ON AN INTERNET BLACKOUT. A NOVELIST NEEDS HIS SOLITUDE TO WORK.
HUGS AND KISSES,
HARRY TRUMAN

Without the wireless service, he had to search for the USB cable to connect the computer to the printer. He printed out the letter, adding his signature in his curliest handwriting. He found a yellowed envelope in the junk drawer and hand-addressed it to the editor who had replaced the one who contracted him in the first place.

He licked the flap, sealed the envelope, and threw it on the table. He didn't have a stamp, so it would have to wait.

Now it was time to get back to the book. No more fooling around.

He called up the document and stared at where he'd left off. It was, of course, the same place he'd left off the previous time he looked.

He was interrupted by an insistent banging on the apartment door. He downed the last of his breakfast, telling himself that he would have been writing that second sentence right now if not for this interruption.

At the door was a small man in a dark blue suit stitched together by light blue thread. It had all the earmarks of an off-the-rack job from the outlet mall. The man had a trial-sized pencil moustache, and spectacles outlined by black plastic rims. He cleared his throat. "Mr. Truman?"

"Yes?"

"Mr. Harry Truman?"

"Fine, fine, what? If you're here to talk to me all about religion or politics, I am in the middle of something very important."

"Mr. Truman, I am an agent with the Internal Revenue Service."

"Is that so?"

"We believe you owe us an explanation."

TWO

Sherman Clayton nervously glanced both ways down the street and jaywalked to the other side. Most days, he would have crossed at the corner, why risk the ticket, but right now he had other things on his mind.

His visit to the honky-tonks on Lower Broadway in downtown Nashville had done little to assuage his nervousness. He reached the parking garage, retrieved his car, and threaded his way through traffic headed out of the downtown area.

The buildings got shorter and a little more spread out as he got to Belle Meade. Knuckles white on the steering wheel, Hank Williams blaring on the radio, Clayton drove down West End until it turned into Harding, and then eventually into Highway 100. That was the thing about Nashville: it was the only place he heard of where you could drive on three different roads without turning the wheel once. He kept driving, past strip malls, past rows of antique shops, past the parks, past pockets of pastureland alternating with pockets of development.

He thought a smoke might calm his nerves. One hand on the steering wheel, one eye on the road, he fumbled for the pack in his pocket and then tried to work out a single cigarette. Two or three tumbled out and went straight to the floor of the car. When he tried to catch them, he diverted his attention from the road and weaved. Someone honked and he jerked upright and straightened the car.

He threw the pack on the passenger seat and drove. He cracked the window for some air.

On the radio, the Hank Williams song ended

and the announcer came on and said a few words about missing country singer Darla Lovell. Clayton punched for another station.

Another half hour and he reached the development called Waterdale Homes. It wasn't anywhere near the water, at least not that you could see.

He pulled in at the entrance and then drove all the way to the back of the subdivision. If the cops ever came for him, he'd have to run out the back door on foot, because there were no roads out of here.

When he got to a particular house, he pulled into the steep driveway and turned off the ignition. He yanked on the parking brake so the car wouldn't roll back down the hill.

Clayton got out of the car and took a moment to spread out the wrinkles on his suit. He was a small, thin man, but impeccably dressed. He wore a hat like he saw guys wearing in old movies.

He went around to the door on the side of the garage and let himself in. He stepped carefully across the garage—his partner often had projects strewn across the concrete floor—and on into the house.

Inside, the man mountain "Bull" Ron Taylor and up-and-coming country music sensation Darla Lovell were sitting on either side of a chess set. More specifically, they were sitting at Clayton's personal chess set, the collectible edition where all the pieces were in the shapes of characters from the Lord of the Rings movies. It had set him back five hundred dollars, and here they were getting their finger oils all over the pieces.

Neither seemed to notice his entrance.

Bull Ron asked the girl, "So, what do I do now?"

"You can move your thingie there or you can move your thingie there."

"Which one?"

"That one."

"Where?"

"There. Or there."

Clayton cleared his throat. "Hey, Bull Ron, can I speak to you a second?"

The two looked up from the game. Bull Ron wrinkled his nose and snorted. "I'm learning something here."

"It's business."

"Just give me a minute."

Clayton opened his mouth to protest, but took note to whom he was speaking and caught his tongue. Bull Ron was, in fact, the biggest and hairiest man anyone in these parts had ever seen. If you shaved him, he could pass for a gorilla.

Clayton needed a drink. Bad. In the kitchen, he went through the fridge. It was full of groceries—that was the girl's influence. But nothing to drink. Not really.

He moved on to the kitchen cabinets and the pantry, but all the bottles he found were empty. He yelled out, "Why are we keeping all these empty bottles?"

Bull Ron yelled back, "Recycling!"

Clayton rolled his eyes. This must be Miss Darla's influence, too.

Desperate, he went back to the bathroom and grabbed the cold medicine and the mouthwash. Returning to the kitchen, he poured equal amounts of each into a glass, and stirred. He sat down at the table and stared at the glass. Maybe this concoction would give him the kick in the head he needed.

He took a deep breath, lifted the glass, and drank it down. It stung in his mouth. It burned all the way down.

He sat back and waited for the sensation to —

Oh. He was going to vomit.

Clutching his belly, he stumbled back down the hall to his bedroom, got to the bathroom, and barely made it to the toilet in time. On his knees, he felt the unpleasant sensation of being turned inside out.

Once he was finished, he wiped his mouth with tissue, and flushed the toilet. At the sink, he checked the mirror to make sure he hadn't messed up his clothes. He carefully smoothed out the wrinkles.

In the living room, he decided to sit and watch the chess match. Bull Ron was daintily moving his piece around, holding it with thumb and forefinger, his pinky sticking out. He tapped the piece down on the board once, skipped one of Darla's, and then set his piece down. He gathered up her piece off the board, and grinned at the girl, exposing crooked teeth. "Like that?"

Darla grinned back. "That's good! You're learning!"

Clayton scowled. He sat forward and gazed more intently at the board.

Darla grabbed one of her pieces and skipped over one of Bull Ron's, then changed direction and skipped over another, then changed direction a third time and skipped over another. She set her piece down on the board and, grinning triumphantly, collected the three pieces she had skipped over.

"Wait!" Clayton stood up. "Are you playing —

checkers?"

Darla and Bull Ron both looked up innocently. Darla snorted. "No, silly. If we were playing checkers, the little pieces would look like cookies." She held up one of her pieces. It was a tiny representation of Gandalf. "This is not a checker piece."

"I know. It's for chess. You're playing checkers on my —" Clayton noticed Bull Ron looking annoyed. "But it's fine. It's fine."

The two returned to their game and Clayton turned his attention to the television. In his absence, someone had turned it on, but clearly to them it was just background noise.

He got the remote and started flipping around. This time of day, there was nothing good on. He got to one of the news channels, and was confronted with the face of Wanda Lovell, tearfully making a statement for the cameras. The sound was too low for him to make out what she was saying, but the strip across the bottom labeled her "Mother of Kidnapped Singer Darla Lovell."

He glanced back at the girl to see whether she'd noticed, then clicked off the TV. The last thing he needed was the girl figuring out things. Hands shaking, he grabbed a sale paper off the coffee table and planted himself in the chair and stared at the various pages of grocery items on sale. He needed to talk to his partner.

He was staring at an ad for pork roast that, if you think about it, was actually a pretty good price, when he heard Bull Ron ask, "So, what's going on?"

Clayton snapped his paper down and peeked over it. The other man stood over him, staring down from on high. Bull Ron towered at more than six-and-a-half feet, at least seven in his boots and cowboy hat.

Clayton said, "We need to talk."

"We're talking now."

"Privately." Clayton took a deep breath, stood, and motioned for the big man to follow him into the kitchen. He glanced back toward the girl and saw she was occupied with the TV. He hoped the girl's mom wasn't on there anymore. He turned to Bull Ron and said in a low voice, "We don't got the money."

"I know. You told me yesterday."

"No, I mean, we still don't got the money. I been all over looking for those guys and I can't find them."

"The homeless guys?"

"Right."

"They double-crossed us? You said they weren't smart enough to do that."

"Apparently, I was wrong."

The girl appeared at the kitchen door. "Hey, can I just go outside? I'm feeling really cooped up."

Clayton snapped upright. "No! Not now. This is not a good time."

"I need some fresh air and some sunshine. I could just stay out in the yard and do some stretches."

"Look, we can all go out later for a burger or something."

"Yeah, but you always make me wear that scarf and those big glasses."

"Please. Just a couple more days. I promise."

She pouted playfully. "Fine."

Once she was gone, Bull Ron asked, "What

would it hurt if she just goes out in the yard?"

"And then one of the neighbors see her? What if they recognize her?"

"Oh, yeah."

Clayton started tapping his fingernail on the countertop. "What am I going to tell the boss?"

"Just tell him what happened."

"Are you crazy? This is a half million dollars we're talking about."

"He'll understand."

Clayton set his jaw. "Think a second. When somebody makes the boss unhappy, what does he do?"

Bull Ron puzzled over this a second. "He calls us."

"Right. I do not want to find out who the boss is going to call to take care of *us*." Clayton glanced in the direction of the living room. Darla was watching TV. "And then there's our other problem."

"What?"

"If we don't get the money, what do we do about her?"

THREE

At first, Truman left Internal Revenue Service agent Marion Russell standing at the door. "Don't you need a warrant to come in?"

The man started to speak, then drew out a handkerchief and sneezed into it. He rubbed his red nose and replaced the cloth into his jacket pocket.

Truman said, "San-kenashi."

The man mistakenly took it for a blessing. "Thank you. Now, if you wish to conduct your business out here, where anyone can listen..."

Truman thought of his neighbors. "Fine. Can I get you some coffee?"

"No." As he came in, the man shivered and rubbed his red nose again. "On second thought, maybe I wouldn't mind something hot."

"Sure thing." Truman went to the kitchen, feeling the need to get something solid in his stomach. If he was about to get audited or something, he wanted a clear head.

While he boiled the water, he found a stale bagel in the cabinet, which he microwaved and buttered. He gripped the buttered bagel with his mouth while he carried two hot, steaming mugs of coffee into the living room. The other man had taken the big chair that was more uncomfortable than it looked. He was fidgeting when Truman handed him the mug of coffee.

"Now," Truman said, taking the couch, "would you please tell me to what I owe this visit?"

"Of course." The man sipped his coffee, sneezed into it, and then set it on the coffee table. He put his briefcase on his lap, snapped it open, and pulled out a manila folder. He snapped the case shut and used it as a laptop desk. "Mr. Truman, it has come to our attention that you have an undeclared source of income."

Truman hesitated. "And why would you say that?"

"We received a tip you were engaging in a weekly poker game."

Truman frowned. Who had snitched? "Well, if you're going to quibble about a few nickels and dimes—"

"And then we checked on your finances, and discovered you recently made a bank deposit of $500,000."

Truman, sipping his coffee, came as close as he had ever in his life to giving a spit-take. As it was, he dribbled coffee on his chin and had to wipe it with his shirttail. "I'm sorry, I would have sworn that you just said I have a half million dollars."

"That is correct." The man dug out his handkerchief again, and wiped his red nose. "And then a record of you making a charitable donation of that same amount."

"Wait." Truman couldn't reach the coffee table from the couch, so he set the mug on the floor. "Did Carlin put you up to this?"

"Who?"

"Jack Carlin down at the paper?"

"I am not allowed to divulge—"

"This is beautiful—Carlin wraps you up as some kind of cockamamie agent from the Internal Revenue Service, and he sends you in with this ridiculous story."

"Mr. Truman, I have to warn you—"

"I should have known better. There is no way that a real-deal agent from the IRS would be dressed like that. Where did you get that suit, from a costume shop or something?"

The little man reached into his coat pocket and pulled out a vinyl wallet. He held out an ID. "Mr. Truman, I assure you that I am, as you call it, the 'real deal.' I would expect you to take this meeting very seriously."

"Of course." Truman cleared his throat. "Actually, it's a lovely suit. I was just—"

"Mr. Truman," the man went on, consulting the file folder sitting atop the laptop desk that was his briefcase, "according to our records, your most recent tax return indicates that your income for the past year was $31,600."

"Unfortunately, that sounds about right."

"And the return you submitted for the prior year indicated that you had a total income of $30,400."

"Fine."

"And then the return you submitted prior to that was for—"

"Excuse me, but could you explain to me where you're going with all this. Telling me that I am poor is hardly news."

"Actually, I have copies of your past five tax returns here with me."

"I'll take your word for it. What's the point?"

"The point, Mr. Truman, is that you have made an enormous donation to the Fifth Avenue Shelter."

"Which is impossible. As you said yourself, there is no way I could afford something like that. No way."

"Perhaps."

"And as an unemployed man with three ex-wives all nipping at my heels, I'm not likely to reach that tax bracket anytime soon."

"Unless, Mr. Truman."

"'Unless'?"

"Yes, Mr. Truman. 'Unless.'"

"'Unless' what?"

"Unless you have been filing fraudulent tax returns."

Truman jerked back and made a face that asked, *Who, me?* Out loud, he asked, "Who, me?"

"Yes, Mr. Truman. This donation indicates some undeclared source of income."

Truman stopped nibbling on his warm bagel. The melted butter was running on his fingers. But he didn't notice that right now.

"My job is to find it."

"Well, if you do, I hope you tell me about it. Because I could use the money." Truman stuffed the rest of the bagel in his mouth. "Any smmfggmmfstmmns?"

"Off the top of my head, I can think of several possibilities."

"Such as?"

"Gambling winnings."

"Okay."

"Sales of illicit drugs."

"Uh-huh."

"Racketeering."

"Really. And you think I'm involved in one of these enterprises."

"Or any number of them." Agent Russell rubbed his nose, and picked up his coffee mug and took another sip. He sneezed into the mug, and set it back on the coffee table. "At the Department of Internal Revenue, we know who you are, Mr. Truman. The kinds of articles that you write. The people you consort with."

"Just because I speak with criminals doesn't make me—"

"We also remember a particular article that you ran in your column."

"You'll have to be more specific."

The man pulled a sheet out of Truman's file. "It was an article entitled, 'CORRUPTION IN THE IRS?,' dated this past April 15."

"Oh."

"That's right, 'Oh.' The only reason you haven't been audited yet is because there are several agents arguing over who gets dibs."

"But you're not here for that?"

The man replaced the folder in the briefcase and snapped it shut again. He set the briefcase on the floor. "No, Mr. Truman. I'm here to find out how you can afford to donate $500,000."

"We've been through that. I can't. Clearly, there's been a mistake—maybe there was a computer glitch, or you have me confused with someone else. I'm not the only guy ever named Harry Truman, you know."

"There is no mistake."

"You know, what I don't understand is why you didn't send a letter."

"Excuse me?"

"Well, for all you know, I came into some money this year—and that would not even show up on my tax return until next spring. But even if you were concerned, the IRS generally sends a letter."

"When this came across my desk, I decided to take a personal interest."

"You should have sent a letter."

When the agent left, they shook hands, Truman with melted butter on his hand, Russell with germs on his hands. After the handshake, both men fought the urge to wipe their hands until they parted.

Once the agent was gone, Truman took the two mugs into the kitchen. As he set them in the sink, he thought about washing out the one into which his guest had sneezed. He decided to worry about it later.

He sat at the table in the kitchen and mulled over the odd visit from Marion Russell, Agent of the Internal Revenue Service. There was something too personal—maybe even gleeful—about the man's visit. Even if the man really was from the IRS, that didn't necessarily mean it wasn't still some kind of prank. Maybe someone at the IRS was pulling strings, somebody upset about that article. And now that somebody was playing a joke on Truman. At the expense of the U.S. taxpayers.

Truman was still mulling it over when the phone rang. He checked the caller ID. It wasn't his publisher, so he picked it up on the third ring. "Hello, you got Truman."

A gruff voice asked, "Truman, what have you got yourself into now?"

FOUR

Sitting at his desk at the *Nashville View*, Jack Carlin leaned far back in his chair, hands locked behind his head, shoes on the desk. He was whistling his own theme music. He thought it was "Eye of the Tiger," but it wasn't.

His mind was on the upcoming midnight vigil. According to his exclusive source — that's how he planned to refer to the anonymous caller in his soon-to-be award-winning story, "an exclusive source" — a member of the Nashville city council would be personally making a drug buy at Percy Priest Lake tonight. Carlin wondered what kind of drugs they were. Carlin wondered which councilperson was buying them.

He only vaguely wondered who made the anonymous call.

Carlin glanced over at the next cubicle, where co-worker and office hottie Tina Davis was furiously at work editing something for the paper. "Hey," he said, "you'll be glad to know I'm working on my next big exclusive."

"I'm sure you are," she replied in a bored voice. She didn't bother to look up from the pages on her desk. Pencil in hand, she scribbled out a whole sentence and wrote a couple notes in the margin. "You're a wonder to behold."

Carlin took his shoes off the desk, sat up, and rolled his chair into her space. "Seriously, you need to hitch your wagon to this rising star. We could be great together."

"Be still my beating heart." Still editing. Scribbling. "You do remember that seminar we had a couple weeks ago, right?"

"Which one?"

"The one where they told you to stop asking your co-workers out." She turned to the next page and continued editing.

"Hey, I'm just doing you a favor. I've got a great lead, and I'm going to have a great story. And when the *New York Times* calls and offers me a huge job in New York, you'll wish you'd been nicer to me."

"I'll take the risk."

"I'm going to be out by the lake tonight. We could take a bottle of wine out there and make an evening of it. The quiet night air. The water lapping against the shore."

"The icicles forming on our extremities."

"There won't be — is it going to be that cold tonight?"

"We do have a weather section in the paper."

Carlin hopped back to his computer and checked the weather for tonight. She was right — it would be cold. With a chance of rain. "Is there any kind of shelter out by the lake?"

Tina turned to the next page and continued editing. "It depends on where you are, I guess."

"How big is the lake?"

"Pretty big."

"I should have asked where I was supposed to be."

"Asked who?"

"An anonymous — that is, my exclusive source. He gave me a hot lead, and it's going to have me out at Percy Priest Lake tonight. I guess I'll have to spend all night sort of sneaking around the circumference. Or perimeter. Is it 'circumference' or 'perimeter'?"

"All I know is, that lead better be hot because it'll be the only thing keeping you warm."

"Not if you also come out to the lake with me. Oh, I see what you're saying."

"Is your hot lead related to the Darla Lovell kidnapping?"

"No, this is something else."

"The chief told you to stay on top of the kidnapping story."

"I'm tired of writing about that. Everybody is reporting on it."

"Because it's news."

"How'm I supposed to stand out if I'm writing the same thing everybody else is writing?"

"The goal is to write it better."

"That's hard."

"Truman wouldn't say that."

"Well, Truman isn't here." Carlin snickered. "But I heard from him."

"When?"

"The goof called with this phony voice, and claimed he saw Darla Lovell out by Waterdale."

"And you're not taking the call seriously?"

"No way that was for real. Darla Lovell's kidnappers aren't going to have her out and about. And certainly not in a fancy area like Waterdale!"

Tina looked up from her editing, pushed out from the desk, and rolled closer to Carlin. "So you're not even going to check it out?"

"No way. I'm not giving Truman the satisfaction. Imagine that, him trying to send me out to Waterdale on some wild goose chase."

"I'm sure he has better things to do than just sit around making prank phone calls." Tina rolled back to her desk and resumed her editing.

Carlin grabbed a note pad and started scribbling down a list of what he'd need for his moonlight vigil at the lake. Rainwear. Plastic bags to protect his camera equipment. Sandwiches. Coffee. It was going to be a long, wet, cold night.

But it would be worth it when he got that story. Then Tina would see.

He thought again about the anonymous call from earlier. He leaned toward Tina's desk. "Hey, have you heard any people saying that I'm not fit to write on Harry Truman's toilet paper?"

She laughed. "That's good. I'll have to remember that."

Carlin was grumbling to himself when his phone rang. His editor, Francis Withers, wanted his ace crime reporter to come into his office pronto. He didn't put it in those words — at least not the part about the "favorite crime reporter" — but Carlin could read between the lines.

With a burst of confidence, he got up from his desk and made his way to the big office at the far wall. As he passed the rows of cubicles, he whistled his theme song, which still wasn't "Eye of the Tiger."

Carlin entered the editor's spacious office. "What's the good word, chief?"

Withers looked up from his paperwork. He was a man older than his age, worn down not by the news, but by the job. "Carlin, have I ever had a good word for you?"

"You will when you hear about my big story."

"Your big story better be about the Darla Lovell kidnapping."

"Ah, everybody is covering that."

"And if you'd do what I told you to do, so would we."

"This is something much bigger, something that will blow city hall wide open," Carlin said, realizing he was running out of breath, but too excited to stop now, "and will make everyone sit up and take notice."

"Take notice of city hall," Withers asked in a slow, measured voice, "or take notice of you?"

Carlin ignored the jab and kept going. "The trick is to figure out who, and what, and where. Once I have those three things, we're square."

"Are you sure you actually have a handle on this so-called 'story'?"

"All I know is that a member of the city council will be out at Percy Priest Lake tonight, buying some kind of black market drugs. If they're doing it personally, then it must be something pretty private. Maybe some kinda sexual drugs."

"You have to be kidding."

"I wonder how the caller knows," Carlin said, mostly to himself. "I wonder who the caller is."

"You don't even know who called you?"

"This is pretty sensitive information, chief. He didn't dare reveal his identity on an unprotected line."

"I think your brain is unprotected."

"You'll see."

"Unfortunately, I see already." Withers motioned to the documents on his desk. "Which brings me to why I called you in here."

Carlin's heart sank when he saw a clipping of his column, marked up in what was now familiar red felt tip pen. His heart sank even lower as he took note of the various supporting documents alongside it.

"I have a few notes here to discuss with you."

"Are these your notes or are these Truman's notes?"

"You should pay attention. They're good notes. They're constructive."

"But he sends one of these packages every week."

"If you would learn something, maybe he'd stop having to do that."

"The man doesn't work here anymore! He's gone, and I'm here now."

"Please stop rubbing it in."

"I don't understand why you can't be more supportive."

"Because Truman was great, and you are not. The only reason Truman is gone is because the boss made me fire him. And the only reason I went along with it is because I'm too close to retirement to start looking for a new job."

"If Truman is so great, why'd Miller get rid of him?"

"Because Truman's crime reporting was making things a little uncomfortable for some of Mr. Miller's friends. And let me tell you, if you were half the reporter that Truman was, you'd be making people like that uncomfortable, too. But you don't make anybody uncomfortable."

"I make people uncomfortable."

"Your column is like a fluffy blanket that keeps everyone warm and cozy so we can all just take a nap until the spring."

"I can't help it if I don't have Truman's

connections. Nobody in the underworld will even talk to me."

"Well, you might make some headway if you stopped calling them the 'underworld.'"

"Do you know where Truman got his information? He has a weekly poker game with cops and mobsters."

"I know. Truman's apartment is like Switzerland."

Carlin snickered. "But I got Truman."

Withers furrowed his brow. "What do you mean?"

"I called the IRS on him. Maybe the cops don't want to stop his poker game, but I just bet he never reports it on his taxes."

"Carlin, you're a jerk."

"Apparently, that's what it takes to make it in this business."

Withers looked at Carlin a second. "Maybe. If you would only channel some of that into your crime column."

The rest of the meeting with the editor was focused on the care package sent by Truman. By the end of the session, Carlin was given an assortment of grammar corrections; a transcript of a fresh interview Truman had conducted with a source that, Truman claimed, Carlin should have quoted in his column; and a spreadsheet outlining how the numbers used in Carlin's story actually contradicted the point he had made.

When Carlin finally got out of there, he was mad enough to spit. But he felt better when he turned his thoughts to his upcoming moonlight vigil out at Percy Priest Lake. He would catch a city council member in the act of buying black market substances. He'd get a big, fat scoop out of it. And then he'd show Tina. He'd show Withers.

And, best of all, he'd show Truman.

He reached Tina's desk. "You know, this story is going to win me a Peabody."

"You mean a Pulitzer."

"Then what's a Peabody?"

"It's the dog with the glasses."

"But it's also an award, right?"

"Yeah—for radio and television."

Carlin went to his desk. He checked his watch. He just had a couple hours to buy a new umbrella, a raincoat, a cooler, a camping lantern, some plastic sandwich bags, and a telescopic lens for his camera.

He chuckled evilly and said to himself, "And then Truman will be the one getting the corrections."

He wasn't sure what that was supposed to mean, but it felt good to say it.

FIVE

The man on the phone was Mike Wagner, a Lt. Detective down at the police department. He was a friend and news source, one of the few who stood by Truman when the ax fell.

"So," Truman asked, "what is her name, and how many months?"

"Hardy har. Are you keeping busy?"

"Well, the new career as a novelist really suits me well. I think it really plays to my strengths."

"Really? How far did you get?"

"'The night was dark.'"

"What's that, the title?"

"The first sentence."

"Classy. What happens after that?"

"No idea."

"You're kidding me. You only got the one sentence?"

"When you reach perfection right out of the gate, why try to top that?"

"No fooling."

"So, seriously, what was the trouble?"

"Which trouble?"

"My trouble."

"Oh, right. That. Yeah, apparently, your name has been getting passed around among certain people."

"What kind of people?"

"Federal people."

"If you're talking about the Internal Revenue Service, they've already come and gone."

"The IRS?"

"Right. A bureau of the Department of the

Treasury. I still don't understand why they didn't send a letter. It's weird enough they paid a visit, but to now report me to the police like this..."

"Wow. So, that now makes two government agencies heard from."

"What, the Environmental Protection Agency is filing a complaint? I swear the septic tank was like that when I got here."

"No, man, the FBI. The Feds have been buzzing around the offices lately. And somewhere between here and there, I heard your name floating around."

"In what context?"

"I'm asking you. So, what *have* you gotten yourself into?"

Truman sighed. "I wish I knew."

After he got off the phone, Truman had to think. What would the FBI be worried about? He hadn't given them any bad press in months. Not since the thing with the dog.

And then there was this other thing with the IRS. The man claimed that Truman had donated a large sum of money to, what was it, the Fifth Avenue Shelter.

Wait.

Truman went to the wastebasket. On hands and knees, he dug through the scraps of paper and rotted banana peels and his empties. Finally, he turned the basket over and scattered its contents on the floor. He sifted through the contents, wishing he had been more conscientious about his refuse. He should probably think more about recycling. But then, saving the world was the last thing on his mind right now.

And there it was: The letter from the local

charity. The one he had savagely folded into the lumpy paper airplane. It was from the Fifth Avenue Shelter.

He ripped open the envelope and found a letter and a card and a flyer. He took them back to the table in the kitchen and flattened the letter with the heel of his right hand. Then he did the same for the card, and for the flyer.

He read the letter. It was addressed to Harry Truman. It thanked him for his generous donation.

He looked at the card. It was a receipt for his donation. Of $500,000.

He looked at the flyer. It explained what the Fifth Avenue Shelter was all about.

He spread the three pieces out on the table and stared. How could this be possible? If this was a joke, it was pretty elaborate. These pieces looked authentic.

He took the letter and held it up to the light. If this were counterfeit, he would have no clue. In fact, holding it up to the light like this was entirely a waste of his time. He squinted, but the act of squinting did nothing to improve his expertise.

He set it down and picked up the card. He thought about wasting his time with that one, too, but the kitchen light was starting to hurt his eyes.

There was only one way for him to figure out whether these were for real. He needed to go down to the Fifth Avenue Shelter.

SIX

"Listen, friend, little Darla Lovell needs your support now more than ever." Buddy Powell, the big boss at Unicorn Stinger Records, was on the phone with a country music radio programmer in Houston. "While we wait for the news that she has finally been released from those dastardly kidnappers."

"Buddy, we're already playing the song every shift."

"I can't help but think of that poor little girl, helpless, sitting somewhere in the dark wondering if she'll ever see her momma again. And I just know that every time some fine radio station like yours plays her new single, it gives her the strength to keep going."

"But she might not even have a radio."

"I'm speaking spiritually, son."

"Oh."

"I know in my heart that every country music station in America wants to see Darla Lovell get home safe-and-sound. And I also know that your listeners are worried about her homecoming, too."

"Well, we do get requests for her song every time they talk about her on the news."

"Well, then."

"So this hasn't hurt business any, has it?"

"Excuse me?"

"The kidnapping. It seems like the longer it takes for Darla Lovell to be released—"

"Are you suggesting that we would exploit that dear girl's predicament? If anything, this is our way of burning the candle in the window."

"Fine."

"Our way of tying a yellow ribbon around the old oak tree."

"Okay. I'm sorry."

"So can we count on you to bump up the number of spins on Darla's new single? Just to show we all want her home safely?"

There was a pause. "Well, I guess we could move a few things around on the schedule. We may be able to get her up to a dozen times a day."

"Sixteen a day would be more helpful."

"I don't know, Buddy…"

"When this is all said and done, and Darla is home safe with her momma, I want to be able to say that your fine radio station helped her get there."

"Gah! Fine."

Once Buddy got off the phone, he scribbled the number 16 next to the station's call letters on his list. All the major markets were accounted for—and once those stations reported their playlists, Darla Lovell's debut single, "Baby Got Home," would see a nice bump in its chart position next week. All the other country music outlets across the nation would then follow suit.

Buddy ran out in the front office. The FBI man, Special Agent Andrew Reed, looked up from his magazine. Buddy gave him a cursory wave. "How ya doing?" Without waiting for an answer, he turned to his assistant. "Margie? I just got an idea—how quickly can we get a few thousand yellow ribbons?"

She blinked. "Ribbons?"

"Yeah. And get 'em printed with something like 'Welcome home, Darla Lovell.' We'll need 'em shipped out a case at a time to all the key radio stations. They can all hold a 'Welcome Home, Darla' campaign in their own cities."

"Okie-doke, Mister Powell."

"Let me know." Buddy turned to the FBI man and winked. "We'll give Darla a homecoming she'll never forget."

"Mr. Powell? I see you're still talking to the press about the case. I really think you want to be careful about making so much noise in public while the case is still ongoing."

"I asked the media to respect our privacy. Can I help it if the press keeps hounding me?"

"But you're the one who keeps calling them."

"Not every time."

"You held a press conference."

"What's the problem? I just want to make sure nobody forgets our poor little angel while she's out there in some strange place freezing in the dark. You know?"

"I just recommend that you cool it. At least, until Miss Lovell is home safe."

"Thank you for your concern. If you need me, I'll be in my office doing some work."

Margie waved a note. "By the way, Mrs. Lovell left a message while you were on the phone."

Buddy snatched the note out of her hand, frowned at it, and went into his office. He shut the door. He got a cell phone out of his desk drawer, and took it into his private washroom. He shut that door, too. He turned on the water. He called Darla's momma, Wanda Lovell.

On the second ring, she picked up. "Hello?"

"This is Buddy."

"What number you calling from?"

"This is one of those what you call 'disposable

cell phones.'"

"What for?"

"Because the FBI has the office phone tapped, and for all I know got my personal phone tapped, too."

"Why would they do that?"

"Because they are trying to catch the kidnappers, dummy. Don't you watch the movies?"

"Not those kinda movies."

"Fine. So, Margie says you called?"

"Yes. When should I expect Darla home? The reason I ask is I got soup on."

Buddy frowned. "You haven't already heard from the Feds or nobody?"

"No."

"Huh." He checked his genuine imitation Rolex watch. "According to the schedule, she should have got there by now. She should be along any time."

"Good."

"Now you remember what I said, right? About her not talking to nobody?"

"Right."

"I don't want that girl saying anything about her experiences until we get a chance to explain some things to her."

"I remember all that, Buddy. As soon as she gets here and we have our soup, we'll go and take ourselves a vacation out in the mountains where nobody can find us. We'll wait for you there and you can talk to her all about it."

"That's fine." After he got off the phone, Buddy turned off the water and opened the door to his office. He was shocked to see he wasn't alone.

FBI Special Agent Charles Murphy was spinning

himself in Buddy's own office chair. Reed stood watching.

Buddy attempted to hide his annoyance. "Well! You've brought good news, I take it?"

Murphy lowered his shoes and stopped spinning. Face turning red, he said, "I'm afraid not."

"What? There ain't? What happened?" Buddy collected himself. "That is, I mean—what happened?"

"No need to be alarmed, Mr. Powell. The drop was made without a hitch."

"While we were unable to apprehend anybody," Reed added, "that also means they got the money. So there's no reason for them not to go through with the exchange."

Buddy frowned. "But the exchange was supposed to have happened already."

Reed held out his hands. "Please, let me assure that the FBI is doing everything we can. There is every possibility of her safe return."

"That is," Murphy added, "if they haven't done something horrible."

"What do you mean?"

"Well, there was this one case where they had already left the victim buried in this bunker, with just enough—"

"I'm sure nothing like that happened to Miss Lovell," Reed cut in. "She'll be fine. Don't you worry."

Murphy turned to Reed. "Hey, remember that case where they sent the victim back a piece at a time?"

Reed, eyes wide, turned to Buddy. "Which is not what's going to happen here!"

"Well," Murphy said, "it could happen."

"But it probably won't."

"Probably."

"Won't."

"Right, probably won't." Murphy turned to Buddy. "But just so you're prepared, sir, it could. You just don't know what these low-lifes are capable of."

Reed said, "Just relax, Mr. Powell. It is too early to start assuming the worst. For all we know, Miss Lovell is being dropped off right now. And then we'll just have a few words with her —"

"You're gonna talk to her?"

"Of course. She's been through an ordeal, of course, so we will make sure she gets all the medical attention and counseling she needs. But we also need to find out anything she can tell us about her captors while the trail is hot."

Buddy plopped down into his now vacant office chair. "I-I was just hoping she'd get a chance to go away with her momma before anyone spoke with her. You know, so she gets the rest she needs."

Reed smiled. "Rest assured, we will respect her health and her state of mind. We have her best interests at heart."

Buddy licked his lips. "I'm sure you do."

Margie buzzed him. "Sherman is here to see you."

Buddy choked, his face losing the last of its color. "Excuse me, gentlemen." He forced a chuckle. "This is record company business."

He shot out to the waiting area, where Clayton was seated on the couch. Buddy motioned for the man to follow him outside, where they walked briskly along the sidewalk down Music Row. Twice, Clayton started to say something, but Buddy cut him off.

A block away, in the parking lot for a local recording studio, Buddy clipped off the end of a cigar and lit it. Once he finished puffing, he turned on Clayton. "What are you thinking, coming into the office like that right now?"

"What do you mean? I'm a regular employee, ain't I?"

"Yeah, I guess. But it just don't seem smart right now. Anyway, don't bring Darla home quite yet. I just found out the Feds are planning to talk to her."

"Well, of course they want to talk to her. They want to find out what they can about the kidnappers while the trail is still hot."

"I didn't know they were planning to whisk her off as soon as she came in. I thought I'd get a chance to talk to her first. You know, explain some things."

"What's the problem? Go talk to her now."

Buddy spat on the pavement. "With all these Feds following me around?"

"Surely we can get you out to the house without them seeing you."

"So, what happened? Why hadn't you dropped off Darla?"

"That's what I came to talk to you about. There's a problem with the money."

"What about the money?"

"We don't got it."

Buddy choked. "What do you mean you don't got it?"

"I mean we don't got it."

"But that's my money!"

"I know, Mr. Powell."

"So, what happened to it?"

"That's it. I don't know. We had our, er, temporary employees all set to do the pick-up for us—you know, set 'em up to stand in as the kidnappers."

"Them homeless guys made off with the money?"

Clayton fiddled with his tie. "Must have. They disappeared. Nobody seen 'em."

"And they got away with my money? A half million dollars?"

"Well, it's not like it was your own money."

"What do you mean it's not my money, of course, it's my money! I been paying on the insurance policy, fair and square, so I got that payoff coming to me! And I am not about to lose out because you and that gorilla done thrown it away down at the homeless shelter."

"Maybe we could ask for another ransom."

"Another—?" Buddy sputtered. "Are you insane, boy?"

"Why not?"

Buddy puffed his cigar and paced in the parking lot. "Well, maybe I should look into it."

"Sure."

"But in the meantime, you keep Darla out of sight. We can't have her show up yet."

"Yes, boss."

"I'll try to get out to the house and have a talk with her. But we gotta be careful—I got FBI guys crawling all over my backside."

"Yes, sir."

"And you find where them homeless guys got to

and get my money!" Buddy threw his cigar on the blacktop and squished it out with the toe of his leather boot. He walked back to the office alone.

Inside, there were now a half dozen FBI agents in the waiting room, all buzzing. One of them was presenting a printout to Murphy. "The exact same amount of money was deposited in a bank account belonging to one Harry Truman. Like the president. He used to write a column for the newspaper in town here."

Murphy snatched the paper out of the other man's hand. He growled, "I know who he is."

"Hey," Reed said, "is he the one with the dog?"

SEVEN

As one would imagine, the Fifth Avenue Shelter was down on, well, Fifth Street—five blocks from the river, in fact.

Thanks to some free wireless at the local branch of a particular fast food chain, Truman had looked up the mission's official website. The charity's stated goals were to meet the needs of men, women, and women with children in urgent need of shelter—food, clothing, running water, and a place to sleep. The mission also offered recovery programs, and educational opportunities.

There was also some mention of a spiritual agenda, as a means to help people to "find fulfillment in life" and to "become a positive part of their community." The site included a six-point checklist for the mission's statement of faith.

Within a good five or six blocks were many of the amenities you'd find in a healthy, medium-sized city: the convention center, the hockey arena, the bus station, plus clusters of venues, restaurants, and businesses.

Truman drove around in big circles looking for free parking that wouldn't get him ticketed or towed. Giving up on that, he started looking for any vacancies in the pay lots. He long ago figured out that if you want to make your fortune in Nashville, the real money must be in parking lots.

He found a spot in an open-air pay lot on Eighth Street, three blocks away from the mission. He reached for the paper bag sitting on the passenger seat, and pulled out his purchases from his stop at the costume shop: A fake moustache and matching glue. He applied the glue lightly—he didn't want to run into any skin-related disasters later—and then patted the moustache into place. He checked his job in the rearview mirror. He smiled, and the moustache did not fall off.

Not a bad look for him.

He locked up the car, and walked in ever-widening circles until he discovered where you put your money. It was a big contraption with a lot of numbered slots for inserting folded money. He only had a few bucks, so he paid an hour's worth. He didn't exactly know what would happen to the car if he was late, but he was in no hurry to find out.

He walked the few blocks to the mission, crossing the street twice to avoid a construction zone. Every few yards, he touched his moustache again.

In front of the shelter, three men milled about in unseasonably warm overcoats and woolen hats. They didn't seem headed anywhere in particular, did not seem to be interacting in any way. As Truman reached the door, they moved away to give him his space. Only one of them even glanced at Truman, and that one turned up his collar and turned away.

Inside, the front desk greeted incoming traffic, which had a choice of the hall to the right or the hall to the left. The man behind the desk looked up from his reading. "Hello! How may we help you?"

Truman grinned his mustachiest smile. "Hello! I believe you are expecting me."

"And you are—?"

"Martin Van Buren, with the Allied All-Saints Charity Fund Exploration Committee. I've been sent to inspect your facility to determine that it is up to AACFEC standards."

"Oh!" The man leaped for the phone, punched a button, and spoke into the handset. "Geneva, there's someone here to see you. A Mr. — ?"

"Martin Van Buren."

"A Mr. Van Buren. With the Allied...um — "

"Allied All-Saints Charity Fund Exploration Committee."

"Some committee." The man listened a second, then thanked the other party. He set down the handset. "Miss Phillips will be with you in a minute."

"Thank you." Truman wandered the lobby while he waited. A bulletin board, decorated with paper dolls, was littered with announcements, schedules, and opportunities for housing and employment.

Along the wall, a series of framed photographs led up to a sign explaining it was an exhibit. The photos, bursting with colors, featured exotic animals in equally exotic settings. The exhibit was, apparently, a kind of travelogue of sorts from the photographer's trip to New Zealand.

Stacked along the counter was a variety of reading materials — local newspapers, pamphlets, religious publications, and employment circulars. He began skimming a pamphlet on the evils of drinking.

"Mr. Van Buren?"

"Oh. Yes?" Truman turned and his breath was gone. The woman was tall and thin, with perfect cheekbones, and buttery brown skin. "You are Miss Phillips," he hoped.

"Call me Geneva." Her smile sparkled. "What can I do for you today?"

"Um. Yes. Well." Truman cleared his throat and tried to focus. "I represent a consortium of investors who wish to create a list of candidates for large charitable donations. I'm here to inspect the Fifth Avenue Shelter to determine its suitability as a candidate."

"Lovely!"

"Yes." He felt his face growing warm. He fought the urge to check his moustache again. "Well, I was hoping you could show me around. So I could see what my money is funding—that is, what the committee's money would be funding."

"Of course!" Geneva smiled, and motioned for him to follow. She needn't have asked. "We'll start with the Fifth Avenue Health Service."

They took the hall to the left. The photographic exhibit seemed to stretch all the way down to where the hall turned.

"Over here, we have a medical clinic, a dental clinic, and mental health services."

Truman looked through the windows at a series of waiting rooms. "That sounds fine."

"We also offer to pray with the patients and offer them spiritual counseling."

"Uh-huh."

"But only if they ask for it," Geneva added. "We never force our beliefs on anyone. We just want to show them the love of Jesus."

Truman pursed his mustachioed lips. "Hm-mm."

"And down here we have our mission facilities." Geneva led him down to a separate section. She opened a set of double doors to a gymnasium. A group of men were playing half-court basketball. "Here's the gym. During emergency situations, we can also set up extra cots in here."

Truman nodded toward the game. "No kids in here?"

"They'd be in school this time of day."

"Oh. Right."

One of the men playing basketball signaled for Geneva's attention. She smiled at Truman, "Excuse me a moment."

As she walked off, Truman watched. He was startled when someone entering bumped into him. He turned around and was suddenly confronted with a familiar face, eyes as wide as his own. The man, Gilbert Dawkins, blurted, "Truman!"

"Shh!" Truman self-consciously touched his moustache. "I'm supposed to be Martin Van Buren. So cool it."

The other man, a weaselly little man with sunken eyes and peach fuzzy along his chin, nodded uncertainly. "Look, Truman, I'm sorry about the check, man, It was all I knew to do."

"Fine, fine." Truman waved the man away. "Now beat it, I'm working."

"Sure thing, Truman." The weasel exited the gym.

And none too soon, as Geneva was walking back. Truman nervously grinned to indicate that his cover had not been blown.

"Sorry about that." She led him outside and closed the gym doors. "Now where were we? Down this hall here are the private rooms. We have two bunk beds per room, so we can fit four stay-overs in a unit."

Truman nodded fervently. He checked the moustache. Yes, it was still on. "I see."

"While folks stay here, we offer help with job

searches, education, and medical care."

"So the kids are in school here?"

"Actually, I meant G.E.D. assistance and occupational training."

"Oh! Of course."

"And then this at the end is the chapel. We have a service every evening, and then Sunday morning."

Truman fought the urge to touch his moustache again. He wondered whether it was crooked.

"And on campus, we also have a working soup kitchen, a full recovery center, and a dedicated shelter for at-risk women and their children. If you like, we could go visit those facilities as well."

"That won't be necessary." With a great force of will, he stopped holding his moustache in place. He needed to trust the glue. "Now, could you tell me what would happen if I were to make a donation?"

Geneva smiled and motioned to the facilities around them. "Well, unless you were to specify one specific ministry of the shelter, your donation would be disbursed evenly among all the —"

"I'm sorry," he interrupted. "I meant, what would literally happen? I mean, if I write a check, who in the building would receive it? Who would write out my receipt? Stuff like that?"

"Oh! Well, depending on how you made your donation, electronically or through the mail —"

"Let's cut right to the 'Thank you' letter. There would be some kind of acknowledgment of the donation, right?"

She smiled. "If you're worried about the tax write-off, then yes, there would be —"

"Any examples handy?"

"Of —?"

"The actual letter. Do you have the stationary anywhere that I could see? So I would know what to look for."

"Oh. Well, there would be some in my office." Geneva motioned for him to follow her down the hall, continuing in the same direction, until he realized they had made a complete circle back to the front desk.

Her office was off to the side. She offered him a chair while she went behind her desk. She opened a drawer, pulled out a sheet of white paper, and offered it to him. "Like this?"

He held it up to the light and looked at it with that same inexpert eye. "I think so. And there's also a card that lists the amount on it for tax purposes, correct?"

She wrinkled her brow. "Uh-huh." She went to the drawer again and brought out a three-by-five white card.

Truman held that up to the light as well. Nothing. "Thank you. And may I keep these?"

"Oh. I don't know if that would be appropriate."

He chuckled heavily. "Come on, you didn't think I planned to take these back to my lair and forge these somehow, did you?"

She frowned. "Not until now."

"Well, I'm not."

"What do you need them for?"

"Oh, these will help me make my financial decision. As I visit the various charitable organizations and, um, collect stationary from all of them, I'll be able to spread them all out on the desk. And pray over them."

"I see. Well, I guess there's no harm in that. Even

if you forged those documents, the donations would still end up with us, right?"

EIGHT

Once he left the Fifth Avenue Shelter, Truman took his blank documents and instead of walking west toward his car, walked east another two blocks. He got to a club, the front of which had been transformed into a facsimile of the very famous Russian tourist spot The Kremlin. In fact, that was the club's new name.

Give it a couple weeks, Truman told himself. Before the paint was dry, the club would close down again, and change hands, and become some other "theme" club for a couple weeks. This part of town, no club would be able to make a go of it. Even if they changed the name to Free Beer and Hot Chicken.

Past the fake Kremlin, Truman walked across the empty parking lot and came to a cement block building decorated in spray paint designs. This was the Union Jack Print Shop, where Truman knew some people.

Inside, the bell rang to announce him. He waited at the front counter, listening to the roar of printing machines. He sniffed the waves of ink aroma in the air that washed out to greet him.

He loved the sound of the printers. But as the technology changed, the familiar sounds would disappear. It made him sad.

Eventually, somebody came out — Bobby Rayburn, a guy who missed the memo that nobody wore sideburns like that anymore. He saw Truman and he froze. His face lost some of its color. "Truman! Wh-what are you doing here?"

"Looking for Marty. Is he around?"

Bobby seemed relieved. "Sure, man. I'll tell him

you're here."

While Truman waited, he wandered the small lobby area. Posters and t-shirt designs were taped and pinned all over the walls. Some promoted concerts, others celebrated specific sports teams, and some simply demonstrated artistic expression for its own sake.

"Hey, man, what's the haps?" Marty Allman always liked to phrase normal things in a way that he thought would make him sound cool. He was often wrong. "I almost didn't recognize you there. You look good."

"Thanks. I wanted your expert opinion on something."

"Surely." Marty was wiping his hands on an ink-soaked towel. "Come on back, Jack."

Truman rounded the counter and followed back to the studio, where Marty had designed many of the posters out front. The place was stocked full of various art supplies, and paper stock of various shapes and sizes.

Marty motioned to his drawing table. Pinned to it was a big sheet of white paper, on which he had been penciling a burly monster in what looked like a football uniform. He said, "This is for a school mascot."

"Uh-huh."

"Oh, but let me show you something else I'm working on." Marty went to a table with a cutting board. From under the table he pulled out a large portfolio, which he brought over and set in front of Truman. He pulled out some oversized sheets. "Take a look."

Truman held the sheets by the edges, trying not

to soil them with his fingers. Marty had created a comic strip—it was completely drawn, inked, and even had word balloons. Truman said, "The word balloons are empty."

"Yeah. That's what I wanted to talk to you about. Maybe you could write something up for me?"

"If you got this far already, don't you already know the words? You had to have already scripted this."

"Yeah, I have the plot all worked out. Like I know what I want the characters here to talk about— I just don't know what I want them to say. I need someone to fine tune it for me."

"If you don't have words, why do you already have the word balloons?"

"It's a demo. I just wanted to see how it'd all fit. Can you write the words to fit in the word balloons?"

"That's a little backward, isn't it?"

"To a writer, maybe."

"I am a writer."

"Well, I'm an artist. I have the plot. I just need help with the words."

"What's your comic about?"

"It's a medical drama. The young doctor there is too dedicated to his work to see that the nurse loves him. And then the older doctor is hiding the fact that he has a terminal disease. And then there's another character, the hospital administrator, who's covering up this dark secret that he is really—"

"A soap opera?"

Marty shrugged. "If you want to be technical about it."

Truman gingerly handed the page over. "And

who are you doing this for?"

"Any of the newspaper syndicates would be fine with me."

"Newspapers? That's going to be a tough sell. They don't really buy comic strip dramas anymore. Not new ones."

"Well, once you help me fine tune the dialogue, you could use some of your inside connections at the newspaper to help me get in front of the right people."

"Haven't you heard? I don't have any inside connections anymore."

"Oh. What'd you do?"

"It's a long story."

"Well, anyway, you could still help me with the dialogue."

"Sorry, my friend, I'm all tied up with my novel."

"You're writing a novel?"

"Have been for four months."

"How's it going?"

"It a great creative outlet. Say, have you thought about doing your series as a webcomic? You know, online?"

"That's generally where webcomics go. On the web."

"Have you thought about it?"

"I don't know." Marty scratched his shaved head with the thin handle of an inking brush. "I really had my heart set on the newspapers."

"You're living in the wrong era. You might as well decide you want to start a swing band."

"There are still swing bands out there. Somewhere."

"Not in the newspapers, there aren't. What I'm saying is, you got to adapt."

"Yeah." Marty sighed. "I guess the future belongs to those who adapt."

"That's exactly what I'm saying."

"And how about you. Are you adapting?"

"I need your help with something," Truman said, dodging the question. He pulled out two sets of papers — the ones he received in the mail, and the blank ones he just got at the Fifth Avenue Shelter. "Are these two sets the same?"

Marty put on his glasses and, one set in each hand, held each out as far as his arms would go. "The same as what?"

"Each other. Are they the same kind of paper, the same kind of printing? Is the one with my name on it legitimate?"

Marty held them up to the light. Truman hoped he was seeing more than Truman had earlier. The man whistled. "You donated $500,000?"

"Actually, I did not. Hence the question."

"So you're trying to pull some kind of tax shelter scam or something?"

"Someone might be. I just need to figure out who before I get left holding the bag."

Marty took the papers over to his light table and set them down. Switching on the table's lamp underneath, he took an eyepiece, something like a jeweler's loupe, and examined each item close up. Finally, he switched off the lamp. "They look the same to me."

"Are you sure?"

"Well, I don't know anything other than the physical papers themselves — but comparing the paper fibers, the paper stock, the weaving, they all seem to be the same kind of paper."

"So they're not counterfeit?"

Marty shrugged. "That's not for me to say. I can't tell you where the papers came from, or if somebody had stolen them, or anything else like that. All I have are these papers. It's pretty likely they came from the same source. For all I know, they came out of the same box."

"I see."

"Does that help?"

"Not really."

NINE

Leaving the print shop, Truman headed west toward the pay lot where he left his car. Walking past the Kremlin—the one in Nashville, not Russia—past the Fifth Avenue Shelter, past the construction zone.

He wasn't feeling any closer to an answer than he was before. This was just weird.

And worse, there really wasn't a precedent he was aware of. If this scam was something that was being pulled out in the world somewhere, this was the first he'd heard of it. It certainly had never been reported while he was doing his column for the paper.

Granted, identity theft was a growing concern in the news. But this was the first case he'd heard of where the identity thief actually paid a deposit before committing his crime.

The other thing nagging at the back of his mind was his friend's outdated plan to be in newspapers. It was a reminder that Truman also had some trouble surviving with the changes in the media.

He decided he was tired of thinking about that for now. So he decided to think about Geneva Phillips the rest of the walk back to his car.

Once he pulled out of the lot, he drove down West End toward his bank. He was wondering what a date with a religious girl would be like, what sorts of places religious people went to on dates, what they did for a good time, when he pulled into the bank's parking lot.

Across the street used to be a bookstore. Now it was a grocery store and condos.

Inside the bank, Truman saw that the cute teller

was on duty. She was currently waiting on an elderly gentleman who was slowly counting out coins on the counter. She smiled at the man patiently as he continued to labor over the process.

Truman was trying to hang back and wait for her, but the young man at the next window was too on the ball. "May I help you, sir?"

Truman glanced at the girl, at the old man, then decided what the heck. He went up to the window and smiled. "Hi."

The teller greeted him. "Hello. How are you today?"

"Fine, thanks." Truman looked over at the next window and the cute girl saw him. He smiled. "Hello!"

She smiled back. "Hello, Mr. Truman. That's a nice look for you!"

"How's that?"

"The moustache is new, isn't it?"

"Oh." Truman reached up and peeled it off. "I was at a costume luncheon." Embarrassed, he turned to the young man at his own window. "Listen, I wanted to check on recent transactions in my checking account."

"Could you give me your account number, sir?"

"Ah." Truman, who had never even tried to memorize his account number, dug out his wallet in hopes of finding an old deposit slip. Then he remembered that he had his checkbook in the pocket of his jacket. He had only recently started carrying it around—without his company job, he no longer had a company credit card. (Not counting the one he "borrowed" from his old boss at the paper—and that was just for special occasions.) "Here."

The young man opened the checkbook and, reading the numbers off the top check, keyed them into his terminal. He looked at the screen. "All right, now what are you looking for?"

"Whether there were any large deposits, followed by any large withdrawals."

"On the 10th, there was a deposit of $500,000. Is that what you mean?"

"I think that would qualify."

"And then, ten days later, a check for that amount was cashed."

"Cashed? You mean, someone came in here and cashed a check?"

"No, the funds were transferred to another banking institution."

"Can you tell me who the check was written out to? In fact, could you just print me out a whole list of all my recent transactions?"

"It sounds like maybe you'd like to speak with one of our associates."

"Aren't you an associate?"

"I mean one of our associates over there." The young man pointed to the offices on the other side of the foyer. "They'll be able to help you with your needs."

"Thank you." Truman crossed over to the other side and found a desk occupied by a rather large woman, her hair pulled up into a spring-loaded bun.

She greeted him in a thick, German accent, "Allo! May I help you?"

"Allo, I mean, hello." He took a chair. "I wanted to check on recent transactions. First, there was apparently a large sum that was deposited into my account without my knowledge or consent, and then a large sum that was withdrawn without my knowledge or consent. Can we check on that?"

"Please you tell me your account number, sir?"

Truman handed her the checkbook, and she punched in the numbers. "All right, and which transactions are you inquiring about?"

"I was told that at some point, I had half a million dollars that someone put into my account, and then someone took that half a million back out again."

"Ja, there was a deposit on the 10th, and then there was a check cashed on the 20th."

"So that happened."

"Ja."

"It's not a computer glitch of some sort? Not some phantom transaction?"

The woman typed on the keyboard and watched the screen. "We have a scan of the deposit slip. It was hand written."

"Can I see it?"

She reached up and turned the monitor toward him. There, on the screen, was the slip. Someone had printed out, by hand, his account number. And, by hand, filled in the amount.

$500,000. Cash.

Truman sat back. "So, he or she must have written down the wrong account number. What happens then?"

"Once they report it, the funds would simply be transferred to the correct account."

"Is that what happened?"

She turned the monitor back and keyed again. She frowned in thought. "I do not believe so."

"What do you mean?"

"A check was written in that exact amount."

"It wasn't a transfer?"

"No."

"But who signed it?"

She frowned and turned the monitor back toward him. "You did."

He looked at the image of the check onscreen. It was made out to the Fifth Avenue Shelter. He squinted at the signature.

Darned if it wasn't his.

TEN

Back at his apartment, there was a man loitering by Truman's door. The man was studiously engrossed in his newspaper, a sure sign he wasn't actually reading it.

Truman picked up the pace toward his door, fishing for his keys. He got the key in the lock before the man pounced.

"Mr. Truman?"

"It depends. Who's asking?"

"I'm Carl Chase, of Mcdonald, Fletcher, and Chase."

"Folk trio, right? I loved you guys at Farm Aid."

"We're your wife's attorneys."

"My wife?" Truman stood there, hand on the key, key in the lock, the apartment door closed. "I'm sorry, but you're going to have to be more specific."

"Mrs. Julie Truman."

"Huh." Truman heard the chain from a few doors down. One of the neighbors peeked out, trying to listen. "Perhaps we should take this inside."

Truman offered the uncomfortable chair to Carl Chase, of Mcdonald, Fletcher, and Chase, Attorneys at Law. "Want some coffee?"

"No, thank you."

"It's no problem, I need some myself. Be right back."

In the kitchen, he boiled some water in the microwave while he got the coffee grounds ready. When it came time to pour, he got himself a fresh mug. For his guest, he grabbed the mug into which IRS agent Marion Russell had sneezed.

Back in the living room, his guest was fidgeting

in the big chair. Truman was all smiles when he offered the cup of coffee. "Here you go," Truman said. "It's a special brew. Old family recipe."

The man hesitated, sniffing it suspiciously. But he saw Truman sipping happily from his own mug, and took a tentative sip. He nodded and smiled. "Hmm. Not bad."

"So, you said you were here on behalf of Julie."

"Yes."

"As her lover, or as her attorney?"

"Mr. Truman, I would advice you against committing libel."

"First of all, it's not libel, it's slander. Second of all, it's not slander if there are no witnesses. And third, it's not slander if it's true."

The man's face took on a crimson hue. Truman sipped his coffee. "You forget, I'm an investigative reporter."

"Were," the man sputtered, once he collected himself. "You were a reporter. But this morning, your editor informed me you are no longer in the newspaper's employ."

"You called the paper?"

"Actually, I went there in person. We were planning to garnish your wages."

"Garnish my—?" Truman sipped from his coffee. "You wanted to offer me a side of fries?"

"You know what the phrase means."

"Sure. But did you ever stop to think what a funny word that is? 'Garnish.' It's one of those words that can be used to mean opposite things." He got up and headed to the bookshelf. "I wonder if the two uses come from different root words?"

"Mr. Truman, stop trying to delay the

inevitable."

"Mr. Chase — can I call you Henry?"

"Carl."

"Right, so Henry, do you think it's fair that I have to pay alimony when I never even wanted the divorce?"

"That's none of my concern."

"I just came home from work one night and Julie had left."

"You had been absent two weeks."

"I was working on a story."

"Mrs. Truman spent the majority of your marriage in fear for her life."

"What did I ever do to her?"

"It's your profession, Mr. Truman. In your line of work — that is, your former line of work," he added, a little too gleefully for Truman's taste, "you regularly consorted with the criminal element. You would bring them home with you."

"I asked them to wipe their shoes on the mat."

"You kidnapped a Federal witness."

"He wasn't safe with the Feds."

"The FBI busted down your front door and shot your wife's dog."

"It got better."

The man gulped down the last of his coffee. "Mr. Truman, it is useless to discuss any of this now. The court granted Mrs. Truman the divorce, and told you to pay alimony."

"Fine." Truman sighed. He pushed himself out off the couch and pulled his checkbook out of his jacket. Despite the absence of funds, he made out a check in the randomly chosen amount of nine hundred and forty five dollars. It looked less fake than a big, round number.

"This is all I can do today." Truman handed over the check to Mr. Chase, who seemed inordinately relieved to have escaped the chair. "Sometime this week, I'm expecting the rest of the advance from my publisher. So, I'd appreciate it if you'd give the check ten days to clear."

"This is not regular, but if it keeps us all from having to go back to court." Chase held the check up to the light and squinted. "But this better be for real."

"Scout's honor."

"That's the Vulcan salute."

"I got a merit badge in *Star Trek*."

"Uh-huh." The man went for the door.

"Hey."

"Yes, Mr. Truman?"

"How is Julie doing?"

The man frowned before he caught himself. "Actually, she recently moved to Florida. She's bartending down in Miami." After a pause, he added, "She got a tattoo."

"Where?"

"Her lower back."

Both men sighed.

Chase collected himself and was all business again. "Thank you for the check, Mr. Truman. And in the future, we expect you to be more diligent about your commitments."

"So what happened to the dog?"

Chase turned from the door and smiled. "I dropped it off at the pound."

ELEVEN

"Wagner."

"Mike? This is Truman. Any word yet on why the Feds are all abuzz about me?"

"Not yet. I'm not assigned to the task force."

"There's a task force? Whatever I didn't do, it must have been pretty bad."

"You haven't kidnapped anyone recently, have you?"

"Not that I remember."

"Then you're probably fine."

"Listen, I need to bend your ear about something."

"Can it wait? Some of us still work for a living."

"Talk to me about identity theft a second. Do you know of any example of identity theft where someone put the money in first?"

"What do you mean?"

"I mean that somebody who was not me inserted a large sum of money into my bank account. And then that same somebody later wrote a check for that amount. So the net loss to me was zero."

"Maybe it was a mistake."

"I don't think so. The same hand-lettered block print on the deposit slip matched the handwriting on the check."

"So someone stole one of your checks and filled it out?"

"Well, yes and no. They filled out the amount, and to whom the check was payable—but somehow they got me to sign it."

"They hold a gun to your head?"

"I think I'd remember. So how about it, heard

anything like that before?"

"Nothing that's come across my desk, but I could ask around. Sounds kind of strange to me."

"On a related note, have you gotten any calls out to the Fifth Avenue Shelter?"

"The mission? Eh, every once in a while we get a complaint. When you have that many hurting people grouped together in one place, there's bound to be some friction. Nothing major, though."

"How about any robberies?"

"Hmm, no. Not that I've heard."

"Uh-huh."

"Is that it?"

"I think so."

***

"Internal Revenue Service."

"Hello. This is the Nashville office, right?"

"That is correct."

"I need to speak with one of your agents, Marion Russell."

"Hold please."

"Thank you."

"I'm sorry, he appears to be stationed in our Memphis office."

***

"Internal Revenue Service."

"Hello, is this the office in Memphis?"

"Yes it is."

"I need to speak with one of your agents, Marion Russell."

"Hold please."

"Thank you."

"I'm sorry, Agent Russell isn't here."

"Do you know when you expect him back in the office?"

"He's out of the office for a family emergency. He's been out since Monday."

"Wait—he's been out of the office all week?"

"Yes, sir. Would you like to speak with another agent?"

"No, thank you. Tell me something—if the Internal Revenue Service has a question regarding an unusual item in a taxpayer's finances, what is the customary way to make contact?"

"We send a letter."

***

"City desk. Tina Davis speaking."

"This is your dreamboat."

"Truman! Where are you calling from?"

"Home."

"I didn't recognize the number."

"It's the landline. I'm not currently using the cell phone because I'm on an Internet blackout."

"Be careful, there's a lawyer looking for you."

"I heard."

"He came in asking around the office. Francis told him you don't work here at the paper anymore."

"How is our fearless publisher? Well, your fearless publisher. Well, your publisher."

"Francis is the same as ever. Always meddling, can't let anyone just do their jobs. He's got me writing a story on a flower show. Can you believe it?

A flower show!"

"Those flowers aren't going to write about themselves. Can I ask a favor?"

"If Francis doesn't find out about it."

"See if you have anything on file regarding the Fifth Avenue Shelter."

"What about it?"

"Just a general overview. News items. Scandals. Complaints. The usual."

"That's a homeless shelter, right? Thinking about moving in?"

"That's not funny."

"Well, seeing as you're unemployed—"

"I'm a novelist now. I have a book deal and everything."

"Your publisher called here, too. They were also surprised to discover you were no longer an employee of the newspaper."

"What did they tell you?"

"More than you care to know."

"Did they talk to Francis?"

"No, I headed them off."

"Thanks. And while you're already bothering people who aren't flower-show-related, could you check whether we have anything on Marion Russell. He claims to be with the IRS."

"What am I supposed to find out?"

"For starters, what he looks like. Failing that, a home address."

"Anything else?"

"Have you ever heard of any case of identity theft where someone actually made a deposit into the victim's account?"

"That's kind of backward, isn't it?"

"That's what I used to think."

"So you're rich now?"

"They took it back."

"Aw. I thought you were finally going to keep your promise and take me away from all this."

"Baby, when I'm a rich man, you'll be the second to know. By the way, how is Carlin doing?"

"Usual bang-up job. He's got a hot tip that has him hiding out at the lake tonight."

TWELVE

At the makeshift command center, set up at the offices of Unicorn Stinger Records, Federal agents Reed and Murphy were holding the fort. All the other members of the task force were out doing errands — some related to the investigation, most of them related to lunch. The label's manager, Buddy Powell, and his assistant, Margaret Schwartzendruber, were also out of the office.

For a good twenty minutes now, Special Agent Murphy had been mumbling to himself as he paced the length of the front room. For most of those twenty minutes, Special Agent Reed sat and watched, his magazine having long been read. He tried to hear what the man was mumbling, but it just sounded like Murphy was saying "Too many, too many," over and over. Reed had no idea what had the other agent in a fit, and he didn't want to intrude.

The two had stayed at the office in case there should be any more calls from the kidnappers. They had tried to convince Mr. Powell to stick around, too; if the kidnappers did call, they would be calling for him. But the man had been insistent that he had an important appointment that could not be broken.

And, frankly, since the task force was currently flummoxed by the kidnappers, it was hard to press their point. They had no idea what was going to happen now.

There had been a kidnapping. There had been a monetary demand. The money had been paid. All that was left of the process was for the return of Darla Lovell. That is, of course, if Ms. Lovell was still alive.

S.A. Reed did not want to think about the thickening possibility that she wasn't going to come back. While the task force continued to follow sparse leads, in hopes of tracking down the men that had taken her, Reed just wanted to hold onto the possibility that she was still all right out there.

Given the FBI's experience with kidnappers, it may not have been realistic at this point. But he was not ready to be realistic.

It helped that he had a nagging thought. "What do you think of Buddy Powell?"

S.A. Murphy stopped in his tracks and stared. His lower lip had some drool on it. "Powell? What about him?"

"I keep wondering if we should keep an eye on him."

"What do you mean? We're here all the time. We're listening to every call that comes through these phones."

"Yeah, but we're not watching him. Not directly. And there are other phones."

Murphy put his fists on his hips. "Whatever are you talking about?"

"He's treating this whole kidnapping like a publicity stunt."

"So? He's making lemonade."

"I asked him to cool it—that it could be dangerous for Miss Lovell. But Powell just called another press conference and kept going."

"That's his world. That's all he knows."

"And then there's the matter of kidnapping insurance."

"What about it?"

"He bought her some. Don't you think that's a

little convenient?"

"Darla Lovell was planning to go on an international tour. When traveling overseas, it's become quite normal for someone worth a lot of money—a potential target for kidnappers—to take out an insurance policy against that very event."

"Buddy Powell thinks of Darla Lovell more as a product than as a person."

"His label has invested a lot of money into her. In this world, she is a product. That's just how it is."

"But she's a person."

"Fine. What's your point?"

Reed shrugged. "Just that we should be paying more attention to Buddy Powell. I think there's more there than we're giving credit."

"I wish you would stop impugning the names of upstanding citizens like Mr. Powell, and pay more attention to lowlifes like Harry Truman."

"Huh?"

Murphy started pacing again. "I can't believe it. I thought I was done with that guy."

"I thought you guys were friends or something."

"You gotta be kidding me. Someone like Truman doesn't have friends. He's a parasite sucking the life force out of all the brave men and women trying to make this country safe for decent folk. He's like a vampire. A life-force vampire."

"But he gave you that nickname."

"And I still owe him for that one." Murphy stopped pacing, and started flexing his fingers in two fists. "'Bow-Wow'—do you really think I want to be known as 'FBI Special Agent Charles "Bow-Wow" Murphy'?"

"It sounded playful."

"Truman starting calling me that in his column. He just wrote it out like that—'FBI Special Agent Charles "Bow Wow" Murphy'—like it was a real nickname. Like people really called me that."

"But you are called that."

"Because he started it!" Murphy's voice had risen in pitch. "He called me that in his column a couple times, and then it caught on. Other agents started calling me 'Bow Wow.' Some were calling me that as a joke, just needling me, humiliating me, but then as newer agents came into the office, they picked it up because they thought that was my actual nickname!"

"Yeah?" Reed chuckled.

Murphy let out a guttural noise.

"So was there some reason for this nickname? Or did Truman just come up with it out of the blue?"

"It was because I shot his dog."

Reed sat forward suddenly. "That was you?"

"It was Truman's fault."

"Uh-huh."

"He set me up."

"I'm sure."

Murphy let out a big sigh. He went across the room, grabbed a chair, and dragged it over to Reed. He sat. He took another deep breath and let it out. "Argh!"

"So what happened?"

"Truman was harboring a fugitive. Arnold Strange."

"The guy who blew the whistle on that big pharmaceutical company?"

Murphy nodded. "Right."

"But he was a Federal witness."

"And Truman kidnapped him."

"Kidnapped him?"

"Well, gave him a ride. To his home."

"Truman's home?"

"Yeah. Truman later claimed he was saving the man's life."

"To be fair, somebody did bomb the motel where you'd been keeping your witness."

"I am sure that we would have stopped that bomb. Or moved him to another room before the bomb went off. Probably."

"Uh-huh."

"But the point remains that Truman had no right to interfere in a Federal operation."

"So, Truman saved the life of a Federal witness. Was the man any safer at Truman's home?"

"It is not a question of safety, it is a question of protocol."

"I bet a lot of people would have considered it a question of safety."

"Who?"

"Well, Arnold Strange, for one. Not to mention everyone in the District Attorney's office. And all the other people whose lives were affected by the outcome of that case."

"Be that as it may," Murphy said, a sour look on his face, "a private vigilante had taken it upon himself to obstruct Federal agents in the course of their duties."

"So where does Truman's dog fit into all this?"

Murphy rubbed his palm over his face, and then continued. "As I mentioned, Truman was harboring a fugitive. We tracked them down to Truman's place of residence."

"Clever."

"We broke down the door."

"Did you knock first?"

"We didn't want to give them the chance to sneak out the back way."

"Uh-huh."

"And so there we were, we had guys there in the full riot gear, ready for anything. And this dog just came up yapping, yapping, yapping."

"What kind of dog?"

"I don't know, one of those Chihuahua deals. You know, all teeth and bulging eyes and noise."

"And you shot it?"

"I shot at it."

"You missed it?"

"Well, it was a small target. And it was hopping all around. It was very unnerving."

"So, a poor, defenseless, little dog."

"It was mean! It was loud! It bared its teeth at me."

"That's no reason to shoot it."

"I only nicked it."

"Wow. So how did all that turn out?"

"Well, Truman and Strange weren't even there. We later found out that they had been a few blocks away, at the house of a cop. A Lt. Wagner. The next day, Truman dressed up Strange as a woman, and Wagner smuggled him into the courtroom."

"And the dog was okay?"

"The FBI was sued over it, and I had to pay for the dog's counseling."

"Counseling."

"Yep. Out of my own pay. Which had already been cut when I was transferred to Omaha."

"Wow."

"And I've been climbing out of the hole ever since." Murphy grunted. "I tried to file a complaint against Wagner."

"What happened?"

"He got a medal or something." Murphy threw up his hands. "And why 'Bow-Wow'? It doesn't even make sense. I mean, if I shot a dog—"

"Nicked it."

"—then that would make me anti-dog, right? I mean, if you're going to make up a nickname, why not something like 'Mad Dog.' Or 'Killer.'" Murphy stared upward dreamily. "Charles 'Killer' Murphy. Now there's a nickname!"

"So, how was Omaha?"

"Actually, quite nice." Murphy pounded his fist into his other palm. "And after all this time, I finally work my way back here and now it's Truman again. But now I've got him with this kidnapping thing."

"I don't see a connection."

"Are you dense?" Murphy stood, waving his arms. "One: There was a $500,000 ransom. Two: Truman recently deposited $500,000 into his bank account. Three: He has a history of being a troublemaker. It's all right there. What more do we need?"

"I would think we need quite a bit more. I doubt that Mr. Truman would do something like this. He's a high-profile individual. He doesn't have a criminal history."

"No criminal history? He's an expert! He's the official historian!"

"Yes, but that doesn't mean he has a history of his own. I mean, one can be an expert on the

89

Revolutionary War without actually participating in it. In fact, I would go out on a limb and say that no expert alive today actually participated in the Revolutionary War."

"A technicality." Murphy swayed a second, and then resumed pacing the carpet. He stopped at the far end of the room and whirled around, pointing. "I'll tell you how this is different—Truman consorts with the criminals. He's anti-authority."

"How do you figure that?"

"He has spent years among the undesirables. Spending time among them. Listening to their side of the story. And in the end, he finally came over to their way of thinking."

"Yeah, but kidnapping?" Reed rubbed the back of his head. "Someone like that would not be foolish enough to put ransom money in his own bank account. I mean, if he's taking lessons from the bad guys, I'd think they would teach him better than that."

"You're forgetting, Reed—criminals are dumb. That's why we catch them. Besides, who knows how deeply he's got in with the underworld? How much he's indebted to them? Has to do their bidding just to stay alive?" Murphy paced a few steps, then stopped, and whirled again. "Not to mention, that man would do anything for a story."

"He's not working at the newspaper anymore."

"He's not? I did not know that." Murphy rubbed his nose. "Then all the more reason to get involved with these lowlifes. He's out of work. Desperate. Will do anything for a buck."

"Are you sure that you're not allowing your personal bias to cloud your judgment?"

"What bias? I know this guy."

"I mean, how did we even get this lead, anyway? He wasn't even on our radar, and suddenly we get an anonymous phone call?"

"It doesn't matter how we got it—look how it panned out. We checked his bank account, and the money was right there."

"Was there. It was already withdrawn."

"Of course it was withdrawn, Reed, try and keep up. Truman obviously had accomplices. He had to split it with them. Or turn it over to his boss."

"That's what I'm saying—if he just got a big satchel of ransom money, why deposit it at all? Why not just run with the money?"

Murphy shook his head. "He's just toying with us."

"Which somehow explains why he gave the money to charity."

"Of course!" Murphy pounded his fist into his palm again. "He's trying to trick us into thinking he's some kind of philanthropist. But I know that's too good to be Truman."

THIRTEEN

Using the company card in the name of one Francis Withers, Truman rented a nondescript gray van. He had to drive four hours to get to the Memphis branch of the Internal Revenue Service.

In the parking lot, he reached for the brown paper bag from the costume shop. In the rearview mirror, he checked his hair, which was slicked back and looked completely wet. He had really piled on the goop.

He inserted the prosthetic set of front teeth. It looked hideous.

He grabbed his toolbox. It was full of tools, but he considered them all just props. After all, he lived in an apartment. Anything that needed fixing was the problem of building maintenance.

He carried the toolbox inside and smiled those teeth at the woman at the front desk.

She failed to hide her shock at his appearance. "M-may I help you?"

"Just point the way, little missie, and I'll get that copy machine taken care of."

"Who are you?"

"William Henry Harrison. Got sent out by Allied Southern Office Supply Repairs."

"But we buy all our equipment from—"

"Yes, ma'am," he interrupted. "They're the ones that called us."

"Oh."

"So, if you'll just point the way to the copy machine. We got a red light at our office that indicates a problem. If you'll just point the way, I'll be out of your hair in two shakes of a lamb's tail."

The young lady got up from behind the desk and led him down the hall to a room filled with office equipment. There was a printer/copy machine, a cutting board, a postal meter, and all manner of supplies for mailing. The drawers and cabinet doors were all labeled with their contents—Pens and Paper Clips and File Folders and the like.

The woman waved a hand at the printer/copy machine. "I wasn't aware there was a problem."

"Well, you'd be surprised how silently a maintenance problem can creep up on you, ma'am. I'll have to check the kind of printouts you've been doing—the type of paper, the amount of toner, that kind of thing."

"Does that matter?"

Truman made a series of impatient sounds, but stopped when he nearly gagged on his fake teeth. "Of course it matters! Everything matters."

"I'm sorry. I didn't know."

"That's all right, ma'am. We'll get you all fixed up. Now, this is the machine that all the agents use for their printouts?"

"No." The woman blinked. "Some of them have individual printers in their offices."

Truman pulled a notebook out of the pocket of his coveralls. He flipped it open and looked at a blank sheet. "How about an agent Marion Russell?"

"He did all his printing here."

"Could you show me to his desk, please?"

"But if he does all his printing here—"

"I need to see what sorts of printouts he has been conducting."

"How do you even know who he is?"

"He's the one who called in the problem. He told

us he'd be out of the office on personal business, and asked that we have a look while he was gone."

"But you said there was a red light back at your office."

"Yes, ma'am, a red light that indicates a call came in. And that we took their order, and are now going to send out a repairman to take a look at the problem."

"Oh."

"So, if you could just show me to his desk, we can get this wrapped up very quickly."

They passed a series of closed office doors to reach Marion Russell's cubicle. His desk was immaculate, except for all the ceramic figurines of dogs. Collies, to be exact.

Truman grinned those teeth at the woman. "The man loves Lassie, don't he?"

"I don't know Mr. Russell's wife."

Truman eyed the desk area, looking for any photographs. "If you'll just give me a few minutes, we'll have this problem worked out in no time."

"I don't think I'm allowed to leave you alone back here."

"Ma'am, I'm a representative of the fine men and women who service all your office equipment." It was difficult talking around the teeth without spraying, but he soldiered on. "We may not dress up in fancy clothes like you desk folks, but we put just as much pride into our work. We work so that you can work."

The woman's face turned red. "I'll just be up front if you need me."

"Thank you. I'm sure it'll only take a few minutes."

Alone, Truman sat at the man's desk. The drawers were locked. The wastebasket had been emptied for days. The In basket was all material related to private taxpayers.

Other than the ceramic dogs, Truman did not see any personal touches in the cubicle of Marion Russell. All he really needed was a photo of Marion Russell to confirm that he was, indeed, the same man who visited Truman's apartment in Nashville.

Barring that, he would have settled for the man's address. Then he could just watch from the street to see whether he recognized the face of the man who lived there.

Truman sat back, defeated. This was a long, wasted trip.

He looked at the dog figurines. One of them was not ceramic. It was a trophy.

Certain there was nobody within earshot, Truman grabbed the phone and made a long distance call.

"This is Tina Davis."

"I got something else for you."

"Truman! Where are you calling from?"

"Internal Revenue Service."

"And you used your one phone call to call me. How touching."

"Listen, Tina, I need you to tell me about a dog show."

FOURTEEN

On the drive out to Waterdale Homes, Buddy Powell rehearsed a look of surprise for when the FBI would finally tell him that Darla Lovell was safely home. He adjusted the rearview mirror to watch himself as he practiced.

"Oh, joy!" he told the mirror. "Our little girl is home and safe! You fine boys have done us all a service. The prayers of America are answered!"

Oh, that last one was good. He needed to remember that "prayers of America" malarkey when the time came.

Buddy smiled at the road. This "kidnapping" scheme was the best artist launch he ever had. More news outlets were talking about Darla than he could have hoped — television, newspapers, magazines, websites, blogs. Every hour, somebody, somewhere, was talking about the tragic kidnapping of up-and-coming country music star Darla Lovell.

Her debut single, "Baby Got Home," was getting played on more and more radio stations. And not just country music stations — that song was making waves at all kinds of formats. Even talk radio was playing it.

And best of all, the campaign came with a $500,000 payday to boot. (As long as those boys got him his insurance money back.)

This stunt was way more effective for the Internet Age than the old methods. In the old days, it was just a struggle to get the top 20 country music stations to play one of Unicorn Stinger's new singles. If a programmer in, say, Bowling Green was slow to add the new single to rotation, then Buddy would send on out his boys Sherman Clayton and Bull Ron to pay the programmer a visit. If the man couldn't be bought, he could be bullied. And, in a pinch, he could also simply be replaced.

So far, that last scenario only had to happen once. Buddy sent flowers to the widow.

But these days, listeners had more options than ever. It just didn't pay to threaten radio programmers like it used to.

Then Buddy found out you could actually insure a person against the event that they were kidnapped. That's when it came to him: Announce some cockamamie international tour, take out a policy on his starlet, wait enough time for the policy to go into effect, and then have Clayton and Bull Ron secretly drive the girl out to their studio in Waterdale. Tell her it was some "rehearsal" time, and a media blackout in advance of her debut. Afterward, if she asked about what happened to the international tour, just tell her you don't want to risk it now. The world's too dangerous, girl. Too many bad people out there.

He fixed the rearview mirror and double-checked he wasn't being followed. It'd be no good if them boys from the FBI were tailing him. That wouldn't do at all. Of course, if he ran into any of them, he'd just say he was going out to the studio to conduct some record label business.

But it would still be better if they didn't crowd him all the time.

The pocket of farmland turned into a lone strip mall. He stopped off at the tobacco and liquor store.

The man at the counter recognized him. "How's that poor girl doing?"

Buddy dropped his trademark executive grin for his weary-but-hopeful face—which also had been practiced in the mirror. "We are still waiting for word from those dastardly kidnappers. All we can do is wait."

"The Missus and I are praying for that young lady every night."

"We surely appreciate that. You got my regular brand of smokes? I'll also need a bottle of whiskey."

Back in the parking lot, Buddy glanced around at all the other cars. None seemed to have men in dark suits and dark glasses. He got in his car, set the bottle of whiskey on the passenger seat, lit a cigarette, made another practice face into the rearview mirror, and got back on the road.

After a few minutes, he reached the turn for Waterdale and pulled into the development. At the house, he parked in the steep driveway.

Inside, he found Sherman Clayton and Bull Ron hunched over the kitchen table. They were having a discussion in low tones.

Buddy growled, "Where's Darla?"

Clayton stiffened at the sound of his boss' voice. Bull Ron simply stretched his arms like an animal that had just finished a nap.

Clayton said, "She's down in the studio rehearsing."

"Good, good. Why ain't you lookin' for them hobos with my money?"

"I have been back down at that shelter, Mr. Powell, and I asked around. They don't know where those men went."

"Go ask again. Take Bull Ron if you need to go bust some heads open. Maybe then they'll remember where those boys are."

Clayton and Bull Ron exchanged a look. Clayton said, "We don't want to leave Darla alone."

"She'd be safe enough here."

"Yes, but she keeps wanting to go outside. We're having a hard time keeping her occupied."

"I see. Maybe I ought to have the girl's mother come out and watch her." Buddy went downstairs. The furnished basement had been converted into a full studio. Darla was in sound booth, headphones on, belting out her big showstopper. Buddy stopped and looked at her. The girl was an angel—long, blonde hair, a nose like a button, and wide eyes a man could get lost in. She exuded a sexy innocence that appealed to men and that connected with women. All the demographic studies confirmed it.

Darla got to the song's bridge when she glanced over and saw him. She stopped singing. "Buddy!"

He gave a little wave, irked that she hadn't finished the song.

Darla doffed the headphones and came out of the booth. She ran over and gave him a hug. "Buddy! I'm so glad to see you!"

"Good to see you, too, darlin'. You been having some good rehearsals for your tour?"

"It's so boring out here. Always cooped up, always doing the same things. Just seeing the same two people. When can I go home?"

"Now, I told you, we're getting you ready to go out on tour. And this is how it is on a tour—one town to the next, from the bus to the venue, from the venue to the bus. You never get to spend much time outside, never get to see many new faces, just singing the same songs over and over. That's what you gotta get used to. If you can't do it here, then you sure as heck can't do it out there on the road."

She stuck out her lower lip. "I guess."

"You said you wanted this."

"Yes, sir."

"Because if you don't want to be a big star, I'll take you home right now. And I'll find somebody else to be the star. Maybe Barbie Carmichael. How about her?"

Darla made a face. "She's a background singer."

"But maybe she'd come out here for a couple weeks if it meant being a star."

"I'm sorry, Buddy. I won't complain no more."

"That's better then. Now, why don't you sit down with Uncle Buddy over here on the couch a minute? We need to have ourselves a talk."

Darla perched herself on the edge of the couch. Buddy, being a much larger man, had to ease himself in. After he got himself situated, he said, "Now, Darla, I'm gonna have to tell you something."

"What's that?"

"People think you've been kidnapped."

"What? Why?"

"Well, there may have been a little bit of help from us."

"I need to call somebody and tell everybody I'm okay!"

"You'll do no such thing. You don't want them to feel silly, do you?"

"But my momma—"

"Your momma knows you're okay. But the important thing is that, when you get out of here, certain people are going to be asking about your experience. You don't tell them who you been with, you hear me?"

"I don't know what you mean."

"When the Feds say, 'Who were you with,' you don't tell them Clayton and Bull Ron."

"But they were here the whole time."

"You don't tell the Feds that. You tell them you were with strangers."

"What strangers?"

"Your kidnappers."

"Why would I do that?"

Buddy gave a heavy sigh. "Let me explain something — this little misunderstanding has done very well for you. Your name and your face have been all over the news. Your song is getting played all over the radio."

"Which song?"

"'Baby Got Home.'"

She pouted. "I didn't want that to be the first single."

"It was the perfect song to release for a little girl that got kidnapped."

Darla's wide eyes got incredibly wider. "You set this all up?"

"Pretty brilliant, if I say so myself. We went the whole nine yards — the ransom demands, the money drop, all of it."

"But what about stuff like phone calls and the money and all that?"

"We got the FBI listening at the label, so Clayton drives all over town, always calling from a one of them disposable cell phones. Then he drops the phone and leaves it wherever he called from."

"And where's the money coming from?"

"It's the label's money, of course." He didn't

mention the insurance policy. "So, you can see why it's important when you get out of here that you play along like it really happened. You can't tell anybody that you weren't really kidnapped."

"Why didn't you tell me any of this before?"

"We didn't want to scare you. The plan was for you and your momma to go out to the cabin afterward and I was gonna tell you all about it out there. But then I just got told by the FBI that they'd expect to talk to you first about all this. But you're not gonna disappoint me, are you?"

Darla sat silent.

Buddy stared, expectantly. He growled, "Well?"

"That would be dishonest."

Buddy sputtered, "What does that have to do with anything?"

"I'm not going to lie about this."

"But you have to! We're committed."

"I can't."

Buddy hauled off and slapped her. The little girl put a hand to her burning cheek, and looked at him with wet eyes.

He pointed a meaty finger. "You listen to me. You are not going to let down your public at a time like this. Unicorn Stinger has made a significant investment in you, and you are not going to throw it away."

He struggled off the couch and stood. Darla silently stared, her lip trembling.

He went up the stairs and he shut the door. He padlocked it.

In the living room, Clayton and Bull Ron had moved to the fancy checker set.

Buddy said, "Keep that door locked until she

starts acting with some sense."

Clayton frowned. "What do you mean?"

"I told her the facts of life and she talked back to me. To me!" Buddy started wringing his hands. "I didn't expect that. Artists always do what I tell 'em."

Bull Ron asked, "So what do we do?"

"Keep her locked up until we have her straightened out." Buddy sighed. "Maybe her momma can bring her around."

Clayton raised an eyebrow. "What happens if she don't?"

Buddy just answered with a dark look. Clayton had seen that look enough times that he didn't need the boss to elaborate.

When Buddy spoke again, he said, "I need you to go find some boy by the name of Harry Truman."

"Who's he?"

"I heard them Federal agents taking about him. Take Bull Ron and squeeze that Truman fella until you get my money."

FIFTEEN

Truman stopped at the red light. Other cars zoomed past him and through the light—one car, two cars, three, four, five. Nashville was the only city he'd ever seen where the red light was considered optional.

Waiting for the light to change, he looked in the rearview mirror. He saw what looked like a familiar car—a maroon Chevy. He squinted to see whether he could recognize the driver.

He told himself not to be paranoid. Which was difficult, since it fit in so well with his worldview. Some believed in a universe that was cold and indifferent. He believed in a universe that was out to get you.

The light changed. Truman drove downtown, almost all the way down to where the riverfront met the Cumberland. In the few blocks that actually looked like something a city person would call "downtown," he got caught in the loop of one-way traffic in the narrow streets. At the crosswalks, tourists loaded down with cowboy hats and camera gear flowed back and forth among the locals, who were dressed in garb that proclaimed their allegiance to one of the local sports teams. A single horse and carriage navigated its way throughout, adding a surreal touch.

Behind the wheel, Truman had to weave his way through the few blocks of "downtown" to find any parking. He went past several garages that were full up.

He finally found a garage that was still taking cars. He pulled onto the ramp, took the ticket, and angled his way through rows of neatly parked cars.

He had to squint until his eyes adjusted to the darkness. He found a single empty spot for his car at the end.

Back out on the sidewalk, he shielded his eyes while they got used to sunlight again. Looking for an opening in the flow of pedestrian traffic, he headed in the direction of the honky-tonks. Take Broadway all the way downtown to the Cumberland River, and you reach a five-block radius that's a magnet for walking tours. When Lower Broad cranks up at night, you can walk down the sidewalk and every four paces or so hear a different local band hammering out some rowdy tune.

Navigating his way through the pedestrians, he followed the current all the way to Charlie's Cattle Call, live music every night of the week. Some nights better than others.

Outside, old Joe "Mohican" was doing his best street musician routine. The man was shriveled from age, multiplied by years out performing in direct sunlight, multiplied by the number of times his heart was broken by another music business executive. Huddled in the cranny between the door for Whiskey Dickens and the door for the Cattle Call, old Joe was hunched over his mandolin, picking it for all it was worth. The sweet bluegrass melody floated by, each note plucked by a lifelong love of the land and the history. The toothless man intoned in a perfect-pitch nasal, a song of bitterness and redemption and a hope that would never arrive.

Truman forgot himself. Forgot everything going on in his life. Others passing by barely turned a head, or at best threw a few coins in the open instrument case. But Truman was transfixed. This was a pure moment, and it demanded all his attention.

When the old man finished, he set the mandolin on his knee and caught his breath. He looked up and, squinting at the bare sunlight, noticed Truman standing there. "Well, hey there, stranger."

"Hi, Joe."

"How are things in your world?"

"Always changing. Got a record contract yet?"

"Not yet. But I keep playing. Them fellers keep coming by. One of these days one of 'em will stop and take a listen and figure out what he's missing."

"You know, with the Internet and all, there are lots of opportunities for independent musicians to find an audience. You don't even need the record company."

"Now don't go on about all that new-fangled stuff with me. I've been on this track all my life, and I'm not about to change trains now."

"Just look at the math of it, Joe — how many folks do you think actually listen to you in a day? Even with all these people walking by, I bet it's not more than a dozen or so."

"Some days, it can get up to twenty."

"Twenty people who stopped."

"Yep, and stopped."

"And listened to a song to the end?"

"Well…"

"Here's the thing, Joe — even if every single person stopped, you're still limited to the number of people who actually pass by. It's a finite number."

"Meaning…"

"If you get yourself on the Internet — post a video, put up some songs — you could reach a much larger audience. Without always being out in the weather."

"The weather does get tough some days."

"I bet."

"It's not like when I started out in 1979. I got to Nashville with just the shirt on my back and this old mandolin in my case, and I started playing on the street that very day. And I just knowed that one day, one of them record label folks would find me here."

"I don't know, Joe. It's all changing now — the music business, the news business, the publishing business — all of it."

"Yeah. I seen it."

"The future belongs to those who can adapt."

The old man grabbed a rag out of the case and started polishing the neck of his instrument. "So, how you been adapting?"

"We were talking about you."

"Uh-huh."

"See you later, Joe." Inside Charlie's Cattle Call, he found the usual suspects. Over at one of the far tables were a couple old guys who, for all Truman knew, were still finishing the same drinks from the last time he came in. Over at the bar, spaced several seats apart, were three guys hunched over their beers and pretzels. Sitting toward the back, his boots up on the table, was a burly young man named Gordon. He was here to keep the peace.

Against the far wall was a tiny stage, a simple block of wood that lifted a maximum of five people and their equipment two inches off the ground. Every night of the week, there was somebody making it work. Well, there was somebody working it, anyway.

From behind the bar, an older lady named Jenny

called out. "What'll it be today, Captain?"

Truman gave her a wave. "Nothing right now, thanks."

"Working, huh?"

"Always working." He kept going until he reached Gordon. The kid kept his boots on the table, his hands locked behind his head, his short sleeves bulging with his muscles, a toothpick in his mouth. Truman turned a chair around backward and straddled it. He leaned elbows on the table. "Seen any good acts lately?"

Gordon shrugged. "Nothing new."

"What's the buzz in country music these days?"

"Everybody's talking about that Darla Lovell."

"Right—the kidnapping. They said something on the radio."

"Man, if I were a record promoter, I would jump on that like it was the end of the world. Know what I mean?"

"I'm not sure that I do."

"I'm just saying I would make hay while the sun was shining."

"I see."

"I heard you got canned at the paper."

"That's right."

"So how do you keep busy?"

"I'm a novelist now."

"No kidding?"

"Got a book deal and everything."

"What's the book about?"

"Oh, I'd rather not give away any of the plot right now. I find that it saps the creative energy if you talk it out too much. Better to keep it all bottled up until I get it down on paper."

"At least tells me how it starts."

"'The night was dark.'"

"Huh?"

"That's how it starts."

"Oh. Then what happens?"

"Ah, you have to wait for the book. Sorry, but a man's got to keep his art sacred."

"I hear that."

"So, Manfred seeing visitors?"

Gordon lifted his head and yelled. "Uncle Manny! You here for Truman?"

A thin voice shouted back: "Send him in!"

Gordon held out his arms. "The boss will see you now."

"Gee. Thanks." Truman got up from the chair, made his way to the open door, and rapped his knuckles twice on the door to announce himself. Inside the small office, Manfred Bergman was crowded by file cabinets that overflowed with folders and loose papers, with shelves jammed with stacks of spreadsheets, and the occasional tattered binder. A paperless office this was not.

Manfred was scribbling notes on a sheet of paper covered with numbers. To make room for his figuring, he had pushed aside the paperweights that were shaped like a computer monitor and keyboard.

At the sound of the knock, he didn't look up. He just waved Truman in while he continued scrutinizing his numbers. "What do you need now?"

Truman, feeling the warmth, took the rickety wooden chair by the door. "Hi, Manfred. I just stopped by to tell you about my day."

"What about it?"

"Well, the oddest thing happened — apparently,

a large sum of money appeared in my bank account, and disappeared before I even knew it was there."

"How much?"

"Quite a bit."

"How much money?"

"Half a mil."

The older man stopped his figuring and looked up, his spectacles fallen halfway down the bridge of his nose. "Yeah?"

"I talked to the bank and everything. By all accounts, the money showed up one day—"

"Computer glitch."

"No, some live person walked in and filled out a deposit slip. They showed me the slip. It was handwritten and everything."

"Who did it?"

"I don't know."

"What'd you do to earn half a mil?"

Truman held out his hands. "No idea."

A curl formed across Manfred's lips. "You did something."

"No, I swear. There is absolutely no reason for this to happen."

"So, what'd you do with it?"

"Nothing. It was gone before I even heard about it."

"Withdrawal?"

"Charitable donation."

Manfred sat up suddenly. His face wrinkled with distaste. "What for?"

Truman held out his hands again. "Again. No idea. I don't know who did this, I don't know where they got the money, I don't know why they gave it to me, I don't know why they took it out, and I don't know why they gave it to charity."

"Huh." Manfred looked off in the distance a second, his mouth rolling into a warm smile. After a second, he shook it off. "So what does this got to do with me?"

"You tell me."

"Me tell you what?"

"Well, I've been scratching my head all day long. I was trying to think, who in the world would have access to these large sums of money. On top of that, who would have reason to hide it in the bank account of some innocent bystander?"

"And so, naturally you thought of me."

"Exactly."

"Look, Truman, regardless of what you print in your crummy column, I run an honest business here."

"I don't have the column anymore."

"I heard that."

"So this is all off the record. In fact, I don't even have the record player anymore."

"Even so, what reason would I have to pull a crazy stunt like that?"

"I wondered whether this was some scheme to launder money. You know, filter it through the personal account of some poor schmuck. Then, should the authorities happen to notice this large sum of money, it's the schmuck who gets all the grief."

"To launder—?" Manfred sat back in the chair. "That wouldn't even work."

"I didn't ask whether the plan worked. Did you do this thing to me?"

"I wonder if it could work." The man began

stroking his chin. "That is a very interesting concept you brought me, Truman."

"Glad to help. So you're saying nobody you know did this?"

"Not that I heard. But you're the reporter."

"Not anymore."

"Oh. Right."

From out in the bar came a shout and a scuffle. And a sneeze. Gordon appeared in the doorway, holding a man in a clearance rack suit by the collar. "Truman, you know this guy?"

"Why, that's Agent Marion Russell of the Internal Revenue Service. Marion, what are you doing here?"

Marion, struggling to free himself of the bouncer, rubbed his nose and waggled a finger at Truman. "I *knew* I'd find you consorting with the criminal element!"

SIXTEEN

Sherman Clayton was wondering how to find a man named Harry Truman. This was a new one for him — up to now, his job had been to visit people for whom the boss already had an address.

Like that radio station manager in Phoenix. Slip the man a few bucks. The Unicorn Stinger record got a few more spins per week.

Or the programmer in Dallas. Bull Ron held the man by his ankles out the window. Once the man got back from the hospital — Bull Ron had eaten barbecue for lunch, so his fingers were kind of slippery — the station added the Unicorn Stinger single in hot rotation.

Then there was the guy in Springfield. He was still listed as missing. His replacement just needed one visit from Clayton and Bull Ron to add the Unicorn Stinger single to the playlist.

But times were changing. All that traveling and bribing and threatening were no longer as cost effective as they used to be.

Clayton turned his attention again to Harry Truman. Flipping through the phone book did not help. He went to the Internet and searched the man's name. All kinds of results came up for Harry S. Truman, president of these United States from 1945 to 1953.

He went back to his search box and put quotation marks around the name "Harry Truman" and added the word "Nashville." A bunch of results came up. They looked like random articles, until he saw the common denominator: These were all the articles written by Harry Truman for the *Nashville*

View.

He clicked through to the paper's website. The street address was listed at the bottom of the homepage.

Bull Ron was in the living room, sitting at the Lord of the Rings collector's edition chess set. Just staring at the pieces on the board.

"Come on," Clayton said. "We got to go."

Bull Ron looked up with sad eyes. "Fine."

Smoothing out the wrinkles in his jacket and grabbing his hat, Clayton went over to the door to the stairs. He pulled on the padlock to make sure it was still locked tight. He listened at the door, but didn't hear anything from downstairs. She hadn't banged on the door for hours now.

Bull Ron asked, "What if she needs something?"

"She's fine. It's like a castle down there. Bathroom. Fridge. Kitchen."

"What if there's some emergency?"

"Eh," Clayton dismissed. "There's a fire extinguisher down there."

***

In the car, Bull Ron snorted. "Ain't right to keep her locked up."

"I assure you, it is necessary."

"Don't see how."

Clayton grinned. "Could it be that you're sweet on young miss—"

Bull Ron instantly had a steel grip on the back of Clayton's neck. "Whut'd you say?"

Clayton struggled to not black out. And to keep the car on the road. He wheezed, "Nothing. It wasn't anything."

Bull Ron let go. "I thought so."

One hand on the wheel, Clayton rubbed the back of his neck. Even on the best days, working with Bull Ron was like working with a wild animal — the trainer can never truly let his guard down. Clayton reminded himself to watch Bull Ron. Because this wild animal was in a mood.

They reached the newspaper offices without further incident. Or any more conversation.

Inside, the young man at the front desk — once he got over his shock at the size of Bull Ron — told them that the editor had an office on the third floor. His name was Francis Withers.

In the elevator, Bull Ron complained, "I thought we wuz looking for Truman."

Clayton, looking at himself in the reflective doors, straightened his collar. "If we go to his boss first, maybe we can catch this Truman guy by surprise."

On the third floor, Clayton looked around at the rows of cubicles. Many were empty, but those that were occupied were buzzing: People at their computers, talking on the phone, or running back and forth with printouts.

He approached the nearest manned cubicle, and cleared his throat. "Excuse me, we're here to speak with a Mr. Withers."

From behind the panel popped up a woman, her curly hair pulled up on top of her head. Eyeglasses hid a face that was probably cute. She looked at Clayton, up at Bull Ron, then back down at Clayton. "Who's looking for him?"

"It's private business."

"Withers never conducts private business in the office."

"It's about one of his employees," Clayton said. He leaned forward and said in a low voice, "A matter of some delicacy."

"Just a shot in the dark—are you two with a collection agency?"

"Something like that."

"Uh-huh. I bet that Withers' answer to your question will be 'He don't work here no more.'" The woman, whose name plate said Tina Davis, leaned back in her chair, pulled a pencil out of the bun on her head, and pointed with the pencil toward the back wall. "You'll find our fearless leader in that big office over there."

The two men went across to the big office. Clayton knocked on the door and entered. The editor was hunched over his desk, marking up a printout with a black grease pencil. He looked up and frowned. "You're late."

Clayton paused midway through adjusting his necktie. "Are we?"

Bull Ron announced, "We just got here."

Withers pulled the cigar out of his mouth and pointed it toward the two men. "I gotta admit, I wouldn't have fingered you two fellas as antique experts."

"Oh," Clayton said. "I think there's been some kind of—"

"But if you're from the Institute, you guys must be worth your salt. Come take a look and tell me what you think."

Withers got up from the desk and led the two men to a short cabinet against the wall. He motioned them to come close and look down at a series of circular objects set on a piece of white cloth. Clayton bent over and squinted. They appeared to be coins. They certainly looked old.

Withers slapped Clayton hard on the back. "My reporter was out in the mountains three months working on a story, and came back with these. What can you tell me about them?"

Clayton held up one of the coins and squinted at it. "Not a thing. We're here about one of your reporters."

Withers' face fell. "Who? Carlin? If you got a beef with his column—"

"No, a Mr. Truman. Harry Truman."

"Oh, for—" Withers stuffed the cigar back in his mouth. He squeezed out the words, "He don't work here no more."

"Why did he quit? Did he come into some money or something?"

"What? No, nothing like that. He hasn't been here for months."

"Could you tell us where to find him?"

Withers took out the cigar. "We do not give out private information about our employees."

Bull Ron snorted. "You said he don't work here."

"That goes for former employees, too. You'll have to serve your summons or drop off your past due notice somewhere else. Truman ain't here, and he ain't gonna be."

The door opened and some old guy in a shirt and tie stuck in his head. "Frank, could you get me those corrections?"

Withers turned and shouted, "They're coming!"

He turned to his unwelcome guests. "So, if you gentlemen will excuse me, we got a newspaper to run here."

Clayton hesitated, his hand back in his pocket. He was not accustomed to leaving a visit unfinished—but they were standing in a giant window in front of an entire floor of witnesses. Their options were limited. Finally, Clayton smiled at the other man. "Thank you for your time. Come on, Ron."

Headed for the elevator, they had passed most of the cubicles when a scruffy man jumped out at them.

"Hey!" The man glanced around and then leaned in. "Did I hear right? You fellas trying to get some money out of Harry Truman?"

A woman's voice sang out, "Jack! Weren't you just leaving to do a story?"

The man batted off the voice as if it were flying around his ear. "Shut up, Tina!" He glanced up at Bull Ron, then turned again to Clayton. "So, you want Truman?"

"Yes."

Jack Carlin grinned maliciously. "I'll tell you where to find him."

SEVENTEEN

Marion Russell, agent of the Internal Revenue Service, went back later to Charlie's Cattle Call. Now that Truman was on his guard, there was no point following him.

But Truman had made his second slip — he had led Marion to the Cattle Call, one of his connections to the criminal underworld. Soon, all of Truman's secrets would be an open book for him to read.

Marion hovered around the entrance, watching folks pass by on the sidewalk. As the sun went down and the lights came up, the honky-tonks along the strip began to kick into gear. Russell, handkerchief over his mouth to avoid sneezing on passersby, was at first a little baffled by the sounds floating toward him from all directions.

As he was buffeted by pedestrians flowing past, he discovered that a few steps in one direction or another had the effect of fine-tuning a radio until you got a clear signal. One step this way, and he heard what sounded like a yodeling girl fronting some sort of fiddlin' rodeo group; one step that way, and he heard a singer with a deep, gravelly voice, backed by a bar rock band; lean a bit to the left, an acoustic folk duo; a bit to the right, somebody crooning Elvis Presley covers. It felt like every time somebody bumped into him, he was picking up something completely different.

Eventually, the Cattle Call started filling up and he felt comfortable sneaking back in. The after-work crowd sported a lot of shirts and ties and even some suit coats, so he had a fighting chance of blending in. He wanted to sit back and observe before he tried again to talk with the young man from earlier. If he could get into the rhythm of the place, he'd have a better chance making a real connection.

The music group onstage sounded like something from a square dance. At least, he assumed as much — in the car, he always listened to talk radio.

At the bar, he had to shout above the music to order a Shirley Temple. The old woman behind the counter gave him a weak smile and mixed his non-alcoholic drink. He took his soda and searched for an unoccupied table in a dark spot.

Nursing his drink, his eyes took in the whole club. A few men and women had braved the small dance floor in front of the small stage. Others milled about — along the bar, along the walls, around the pool tables, talking, drinking, mingling. The chairs at the other tables were also filling up.

His eyes flicked toward the direction of the back office. The door was closed. At one point, the young man he met earlier — the one who roughed him up — came out of the back office, glanced around at the crowd, then went back in and shut the door behind him.

Marion rubbed his nose and resumed watching his fellow patrons. He wondered how many even knew the crime and corruption taking place behind closed doors. Such innocent sheep, eating and drinking obliviously as the wolves made their nefarious plans in back.

A thrill sent a shiver up his spine. Marion sucked in some soda through his straw, took it in a little fast and felt a pinch in his forehead. He needed to cool it.

It's just that his current position at the IRS —

sitting behind a desk at the office—was so constricting. He knew deep down that he needed to be a field agent. A man who went places. Who did things. And that was never going to happen as long as he was an anonymous number-cruncher behind a desk.

This Truman case was Marion Russell's ticket to bigger and better things. When he'd received that tip from a conscientious citizen—that Jack Carlin fellow, a true American—all that the man had mentioned was that Harry Truman was running some weekly poker game and probably not reporting his winnings.

At first, Marion had assumed nothing much would come of it—these games were usually just nickels and dimes, not worth the time and expense to pursue. But when he checked up on this Truman and discovered the amount of money involved—$500,000, imagine! and that was just what he made the mistake of depositing!—Marion knew that this case was big. And if he could nab this Truman and find the true extent of his unreported income, that would surely get Marion Russell noticed at the office.

And if he got some kind of reward at the office, maybe that would make his wife happy. She was always down on him for spending so much time and money on his prize-winning dog, Mr. Mittens. She just didn't understand. It didn't help that the dog show expenses were pushing him further into debt—and it was getting harder to hide it from her in the housekeeping account.

But the extra attention at the office should also lead to a raise in pay. If he could come home with the happy news of a promotion and a raise, maybe then she'd cut her husband the slack a husband needs.

In the back of the club, the young man came back out of the office. Marion gulped down the last of his drink, sneezed into his hand, wiped it on his sleeve, and headed back there. He ambled casually as he could, even as his heart pounded in his ears. This was him approaching a member of the underworld, like something out of Miami Vice.

He navigated his way through the other patrons, handkerchief handy, careful not to sneeze on anybody. He finally made it back to the table where his quarry sat, leaning a chair back on two legs. The young man looked at him and sat forward, bringing the chair on all four legs. "Yeah?"

Marion took down the handkerchief from his mouth, leaned in, and yelled over the music, "We met earlier — I'm a friend of Truman's, remember?"

The man nodded. He didn't say anything.

Marion leaned in again. "Truman sent me over to help."

The man looked puzzled. "Really?"

"You know, I want in on your, you know" — Marion glanced both ways and leaned in to add — "gig tonight."

The man grinned. "He told you about the gig?"

Marion grinned back. "Absolutely. And I'm here to help you any way that I can."

"Great! You got a car?"

EIGHTEEN

When Truman got to his apartment that evening, he found Geneva Phillips waiting for him in the hall. If you were to ask him about it later, Truman had no idea how long he stood there, staring at the goddess at his door. Just that it was an uncomfortably long time, Geneva Phillips staring back at him, her jaw set, eyes blazing.

Finally, after ten years, Truman spoke the first thing that came to mind: "Heh." Not much, but it was a start.

She folded her arms. "Well? What do you have to say for yourself?"

Truman, remembering he was supposed to be somebody else, cleared his throat. "I was just here looking for this 'Truman' fellow. Funny running into you here."

"Uh-huh."

"I had heard that this 'Mr. Truman' had made something of a donation lately to your mission, and thought I'd ask him about his experiences." He rapped his knuckles on the door and then turned to go. "But he doesn't seem to be at home now, so maybe we should just—"

"Your moustache is missing."

His hand shot up to his naked lip. Argh. "Yes, well, I had just shaved it because…because…"

Geneva folded her arms and raised a sassy eyebrow. "Don't you think it's time we stop playing these games, Mr. Truman? Because you are, in fact, Harry Truman, aren't you?"

"Um." Truman's mind shot back to another time he'd blown his cover. He was in Kansas City, playing a waiter, trying to sidle his way up to Duke Cumbee's table. He'd gotten the drink order confused—he never could get the hang of the difference between an *aperitif* and a *digestif*.

At least Geneva wasn't about to tell her goons to take Truman out back for a beating. He hoped.

Truman unlocked the door and opened it. "Fine. Won't you come in?"

Those amazing green eyes scanned the apartment from the doorway. "Are you the only one here?"

Truman glanced around at the mess. Bottles and cans and dirty clothes strewn all over the living room. A collection of dirty plates stacked up on the card table. "My housekeeper has the day off."

"A good girl does not come into a man's apartment alone."

Truman looked around again and scratched his head. None of the women he knew had ever told him that. It occurred to him that if one of his ex-wives had thought that way, it would have saved him a lot of trouble later. "Fine, let's go for a drive. Can a good girl be in a man's car?"

"Depends on where the man plans to drive."

"I'll buy you a drink."

"A good girl doesn't drink."

"Look, you were the one who came to me. If you want to have a conversation, and you won't come inside, then we have to go somewhere."

"What's wrong with right here?"

"In the doorway?" Truman peeked out and glanced both ways. "I got nosy neighbors. Look, how about a burger or a milkshake or something? Or would that also offend you?"

Geneva regarded him a moment. Then she replied in a bored voice, "I suppose that would be fair."

That settled, Truman got his coat. He didn't know what the weatherman had said, but he knew it would be chilly in the car. He locked up and led the way down the stairs and out to his car in the lot.

He drove out of the complex and started up Nine Mile Hill. One hand on the wheel, Truman motioned toward the steep drop-off to their left. "Every couple years, the road starts to split and threatens to tumble off into the ravine there."

"What do they do about it?"

"Patch it up."

"Aren't you scared driving up this way?"

"You get used to it. Besides, I'm the sure the engineers know what they're doing." He wasn't really sure they did, and, for that matter, the prospect of the road splitting terrified him. But he couldn't help but put on a brave face for the goddess with the brown skin and the green eyes.

At the top of the hill, they met rows of civilization — grocery stores, liquor stores, restaurants, shops. In a few minutes, Truman reached the Sonic Drive In and he pulled up to the standing menu with the squawk box. He shut off the car. "What would you like?"

"Hmm. Just some fries."

Truman rolled down the window, and told the squawk box they needed a cheeseburger, onion rings, a cherry-grape-chocolate Coke, and an order of fries. He thought about adding "and two hard boiled eggs," but wasn't in the mood to explain the Marx Brothers.

He left the windows cracked so they didn't fog up. Didn't want the good girl to feel uncomfortable. "So," he said to her, "you figured me out."

"Nothing to it."

"Apparently, you thought it was important enough to track me down."

"Your address was on the check."

"Oh. Right." He cracked his knuckles. "So, how'd you see through me?"

Geneva turned and wagged a finger. "First of all, there was no way that was a real moustache."

"I thought it was pretty good."

"Then there was the matter of that place you claimed to work for—what was the name of that again?"

"The, um, Allied All-Star...lessee..."

"Exactly. Not a real group."

"It could have been."

"Third, you used a presidential name for your cover."

"So? Lots of parents name their kids after presidents."

"Yeah. Yours did. That is, your real parents. And the name 'Harry Truman' was already memorable because of your recent donation."

"For which you have yet to thank me."

"I'm getting to that. And so when this man with the fake moustache working for the fake organization gave me a fake name, I thought it was a big coincidence that two different men would have come through my office with the name of a president."

"Two men?"

"But it turned out to be one man: You in person,

and then you in the mail."

"Ah. So, is that all you had?"

"Actually, I also recognized your name from before. You did a story on my father."

"Oh. Was he happy about it?"

"No."

"They generally aren't."

"And once I had my suspicions, all I had to do was ask Mr. Dawkins about it."

"How'd you know to ask him?"

"I saw you two speak at the shelter. Which was also suspicious—not many strangers from out of town would be so familiar with one of our indigents."

Truman chuckled. "He's been a source off and on for years. He keeps low to the ground, mostly to stay off everyone's radar. You'd be surprised the kinds of things a man can hear at that low altitude."

"Uh-huh." Arms folded.

"So, what did you do once you figured me out?"

"I sorted though my options. I could ignore you. I could report you. I could come to your home and egg your car."

Truman raised both eyebrows. "Can a good girl do that?"

"She can think about it."

"I see."

"So, I guess you get to take the deduction?"

"Excuse me?"

"On the donation. Daddy gives you the money to make your little donation, and you get to keep the tax write-off for yourself?"

"Um. What?" Truman's mind started racing, but the wheels were just spinning in mud. "Wait—who's your father?"

"Doctor Thaddeus Phillips."

"Oh." Truman mentally dug through the files of all his past columns. "When did I write about him?"

"You wrote an article about Phenomilyn."

"Ohhh." Truman sat back, remembering the story now. Phenomilyn was a drug that was being released prematurely into the marketplace. On top of which, the pharmaceutical company was audacious enough to create a new disease — that is, advertise a name for a disease that did not actually exist — to justify the new drug.

Truman's story had brought the duplicity to light, and made it impossible for all the paid-off authorities to continue pretending they didn't know what was going on. He should have gotten a Pulitzer. "Wait, let's back up — so what do you mean 'Daddy' gave me the money? How's your father involved in all this?"

"It's obvious. My folks aren't thrilled that I'm giving my life to the ministry. This is their way of trying to keep control of my life. If I won't take their money over the table, they'll hire someone like you to funnel it for them."

"Isn't it possible I could have just made the donation myself?"

"Did you?"

He grinned. "Well, no. I'm not that good." He saw their server coming with the tray. "Do I tip? I never know whether to tip."

"Yes, you should tip."

He rolled down the window, the young lady told him the amount, and he gave her an extra buck. She thanked him and left without explaining one way or the other whether he should have bothered. He handed the fries to Geneva and took the cheeseburger and onion rings and cherry-grape-chocolate Coke for himself.

"So," he said, taking a sip through his straw, "if your father hates me so much, why would you think he'd even trust me?"

"Because you're unemployed."

"Actually, I'm a novelist."

"And because the very reason he hates you is the reason he can trust you. And because he thinks anyone can be bought."

"Uh-huh. Well, he didn't buy me. I can assure you that your father did not give me any money. At no point has he contacted me. Not about this, not about anything."

She stared at him and squinted, as if that would somehow gauge his sincerity. Apparently, he passed, because she finally said, "Okay."

"Eat your fries. They're getting cold." He unwrapped his cheeseburger and took a bite. Instantly, the ketchup and mustard on his face reminded him why it was unwise to eat a burger in a car with a lady. With his free hand, he scrambled for the glove compartment to find some more napkins. He rewrapped his cheeseburger and wiped his face off. Good thing he didn't have a moustache.

He risked an onion ring, sans ketchup. "So, your parents don't approve of you working among the downtrodden?"

She finished chewing a fry and swallowed. "They think it's beneath us somehow. They don't care that I'm just trying to serve the Lord."

"I'm sure they wonder whether you could serve

the Lord in some other manner. Don't rich people need saving, too?"

"Jesus said, 'Whatsoever you do for the least of these, you do for me.'"

"For Jesus?"

"Absolutely."

"Which is why you're working at the Fifth Avenue Shelter."

"That's right. I want to make a difference."

"Sounds pretty noble from where I sit."

She ate another fry. "So, how did you come up with such a whopping donation for the shelter?"

"I wish I knew."

"What does that mean?"

Truman chewed on his thumbnail. "Would your father have any reason to launder large sums of money?"

"I-I wouldn't know. I should hope not."

"But even if he did, that wouldn't explain the donation. Tell me, once someone sends money to your shelter—can someone somehow get it back out?"

"If it came up, I suppose the person who made the donation could ask for their money back. It's not usual."

"But nobody else."

"Of course not."

"Tell me, who owns the shelter? I mean, when the money comes in, who actually gets it?"

"The shelter is a ministry of a coalition of local churches. A board of ministers watches over it, and then an agency polices them. There's no greedy pockets there, if that's what you're asking."

"Hmm. Even if your board of ministers were

playing with the books, that doesn't explain how they would have dragged me into it."

"Okay, exactly how are you involved?"

Truman took a deep breath and told her. About the IRS agent. About the mysterious deposit at his bank. About the mysterious donation with one of his own checks. "I've been trying to chase down leads," he wrapped up. "But this is all so random, it's like I'm in quicksand just flailing my arms."

"It could be a coincidence."

"Coincidence is just a chain of events waiting to be uncovered."

"So, when you checked the number in your checkbook, what did you find?"

Truman coughed. "Excuse me?"

"Your checkbook. When you double-checked the entries against your checkbook—"

"Baby, I could kiss you!" Truman scooted toward her, and she pushed him back.

"What made you think you could do that?"

NINETEEN

At the newspaper offices, Tina Davis was working on her research for Truman. She had to be sly about it, couldn't let Mr. Withers find out she was doing it. She had her own assignments, weak as they were, as the old man often reminded her.

When Truman called asking for her help, she wasn't all that surprised. Even off the *Nashville View*'s payroll, that man just could not resist sticking his nose into people's business. As such, he called every few weeks for a couple favors. And Tina always did what she could. Partly, because she held out hope that one of these days the man would finally notice she was a woman. But also because, in the event that he landed at another news organization, maybe he'd take her with him.

She had advanced as far as she ever would at this paper. Withers had no faith in her as a reporter. He kept sticking her with little penny ante stories — because, he always told her, if she failed to bring in anything printable, he could still fill those two column inches with something else.

Tina looked at her file on Marion Russell, agent of the Internal Revenue Service. It was thin. The man was not rich enough, powerful enough, or notorious enough to have really made an impact on the news industry. He was just a little man toiling at an office in Memphis, Tennessee.

She had called his office with the pretense of working on a human-interest story, and was told the man was out of town on family business. She asked for a photograph and was a little surprised when they emailed her one. She was also able to find out, via an Internet search engine, where the man lived. He did not seem to have any presence on any social media sites, at least none that were available to strangers.

She used her paper's resources to find a birth certificate and a marriage certificate. Consequently, she knew that Marion Russell was forty-three years of age, married twenty-one years to wife Shirley. No record of any children. However, Marion was active in the dog show circuit—and had spent quite a lot of money on his Pomeranian, Mr. Mittens.

She forwarded everything she had to Truman's email address, knowing full well he was on his "Internet blackout." The next time he called in, she'd remind him to check his email at the library.

That job taken care of, she pushed the folder aside and looked at the next one. It had all her notes for the upcoming Nashville Women's Auxiliary Flower Festival. Tina sighed. She hated getting stuck with these kinds of stories.

But every time she went to Mr. Withers, he claimed she was no good at chasing real leads. In fact, he'd say, if she was good at being a reporter, she wouldn't be asking for stories, she'd be bringing them in off the street herself.

Tina pushed aside the folder for the flower festival and looked at the one she had started on the Fifth Avenue Shelter. On this topic, Truman had requested anything she could dig up—news items, scandals, whatever. She found a couple Lifestyle section items, dating back several years. They were general pieces about helping the helpless around the holidays. She couldn't find any reports of scandal, any misbehavior, anything. That is, not counting one small article about an altercation between homeless men that had taken place a block away; the shelter was only mentioned as a reference point. It did not seem to be in any way involved.

The rest of the folders on her desk were related to various town councils meeting in the Greater Nashville area. Tina let out a big sigh. At most newspapers this size, there would be a veritable army of stringers all spread out across the landscape, each reporting on their little territory. But recent budget cuts meant that more and more of the burden for this kind of reporting came to the main office. Which, of course, meant her. It was all her.

Tina glanced at the next cubicle. Jack Carlin was long gone, probably out at the lake by now. All bundled up, sunk to his knees in mud, hiding in the bushes, waiting for a drug deal that she figured would never happen.

None of Carlin's really big tips ever panned out. He always talked big around the office, how he'd soon make the jump to the majors. He kept sending his clips to the editors at *Time, Newsweek,* and *U.S. News & World Report.* He never heard back, but that never stopped his big talk.

Carlin never even admitted that the only reason he got Truman's slot in the newspaper was because Truman had angered too many of the wrong people. That is, too many friends of the man who owned the newspaper.

More and more in the final months of his column, Truman had turned his attention to white-collar crimes. To corruption among the corporations, among the politicians, and other members of the elite.

Several times she overheard the shouting matches between Withers and Truman. "Spend more time reporting on street level crime," Withers would say. "Nobody wants to read about all those people up in the ivory towers!"

"What you mean is that our illustrious owner, Leopold Miller, doesn't want to read about the ivory towers," Truman would retort. "He doesn't want his paper digging up all the back office deals being conducted by his friends from the country club. He thinks owning a newspaper is a license to cover up their crimes against everyday Joes like you and me!"

"So what?" Withers would reply. "He owns the newspaper, what can you do?"

Toward the end of Truman's time at the paper, those meetings became more and more frequent, and more and more difficult to not overhear. Even with the door to Mr. Withers' office closed, their shouts rattled the glass. Everyone out in the newsroom would share awkward glances and pretend to continue working.

Except Carlin, of course. He'd fold his arms and swivel his desk chair toward the editor's office and watch them through the big windows. He'd grin and chomp his gum and sit back and keep score like he was at the ballgame.

When Truman got his walking papers, Carlin was one of only two in the office who even wanted his slot. The other was Tina herself. Nobody else wanted to risk the wrath of the owner, Leopold Miller.

Tina didn't figure she had much to lose, and this was her big chance to prove herself. Mr. Withers passed on her in an instant. "You can't do the job," he said, with a wave of his hand to dismiss the idea. "You're no good at jumping at a lead."

No amount of whining or pleading changed his mind.

And then there was Jack Carlin. He was idiot enough to think he deserved to replace Truman. And, with no other viable candidates willing to put the noose around their own necks, Carlin got the job. Mr. Withers was clearly not thrilled when he made the announcement, but Carlin still locked his hands together and waved them over his head like he'd won an election or something.

In the four months since he took the post, Carlin's output had been terrible. There were lots of retractions, lots of letters of apology. But since Carlin never, ever went after corruption among white-collar types, there were never any complaints from the top.

Of course, she did not know Jack Carlin's secret. None of them did.

Then, a few weeks in, Truman started calling Tina, asking for some help re-investigating Carlin's articles. She had no idea where his secret investigations led—but she did notice that a big manila envelope would show up every week or so, with Truman's return address. And that Mr. Withers would discuss the contents with Jack Carlin. And then Carlin would be in a very sour mood for the rest of the day.

Tina was yanked out of her thoughts by the gruff voice of Mr. Withers. "Hey, Davis, do you remember those guys who were in here earlier? Big guy, little guy?"

Tina swiveled her desk chair and looked up at her boss. She noticed his forehead was sweating, and his jaw seemed to be clenched. "Sure. What about 'em?"

"Do you happen to know where they went?"

She shook her head. "I didn't talk to them. Why?"

"I'm missing a valuable artifact, and I can't think who else might have taken it. Did you see anyone else go in my office?"

She shrugged. "Everybody. All day long."

"Yeah." He rubbed the back of his neck. "But I'd like a crack at that little guy."

"Carlin talked to them."

"Where is he?"

"Out at Percy Priest Lake."

"In this weather? Why would he be out there?"

"Chasing his big drug story."

"He's supposed to be doing a write-up about that Darla Lovell kidnapping."

"What more is there to say?"

"It's his job to figure that out. All I know is that it sells papers. And something called SEO."

"Search Engine Optimization?"

"Whatever. It makes people look at our website. So find Carlin and tell him to put away his fishing gear and get to work on that kidnapping story." Withers glanced at the folders on her desk. "What are you working on?"

She lunged to cover them up. "My assignments, chief. Flower show. Town council."

"Don't forget the meeting of the Nashville City Council. There's a big vote tonight related to mass transit. And for the love of Edward R. Murrow, record the meeting so we'll have a transcript."

"Right, chief."

"And get Carlin in here on the kidnapping story."

"You know, if Truman were still here, he'd find a fresh angle."

"Ack. Don't talk to me about Truman. My ulcer would be a lot worse if he were still here. Carlin's a terrible writer, but at least I don't get yelled at by Mr. Miller anymore. At least, not every week."

Withers went back to his office and closed the door. Through the big windows, she watched him go to the credenza and search again for his missing object. He checked the carpet, he checked under things, he checked behind things. Whatever he lost, it must be important.

Tina swiveled her chair back to the desk and reached for her company phone book. She called Carlin's cell and got his voicemail. "Mr. Withers says to get back on the kidnapping story," she told the phone. "Besides, none of the council members are going to be at the lake. They're all at City Hall tonight."

As she hung up, Tina thought about the kidnapping of Darla Lovell. If she could think of an angle on this story, then maybe she could finally prove herself. She thought briefly of that call that came in earlier. Someone who claimed they saw Darla Lovell out at Waterdale.

For once, Tina had to side with Carlin. It was probably a crank call, and Waterdale was too long a drive for a wild goose chase.

TWENTY

Truman was exhausted when he got back home to his apartment. It had been a long day, and the green-eyed goddess had made him feel foolish. He just wanted to grab a bottle of whatever was left in the cupboard, drink it down hard and fast, and kill whatever brain cells that still held any memory of the day's events.

He locked the front door, doffed his shoes, and undid his belt. He was out of his pants and unbuttoning his shirt as he reached the kitchen. He was in his socks and underwear when he discovered he was out of bourbon. And the vinegar just didn't seem right this time of night.

Sauntering to the living room, he plopped on the couch and considered his options. Maybe a good night's sleep was what he needed.

Sure, that was the ticket. In the morning, everything would make sense: His unemployment. The mysterious transactions in his bank account. The cold-ridden man from the IRS. The curious news that the FBI was buzzing about him. The plot for his heretofore unwritten novel. Even how Geneva Phillips was immune to his considerable charms.

In the morning light, all would be clear. The truth would be revealed by a bluebird or an angel or maybe even his muse. And if she looked like Olivia Newton John, all the better.

He stretched on the couch and wondered when he got to feeling so old and worn out. When he was still a working reporter, he'd kept way worse hours than these. But ever since he had been fired by the *Nashville View*, it was like he was off balance.

He decided to brew some tea. Maybe the hot, flavored water would settle his stomach and his nerves. Waiting for the water to boil, he sat at the kitchen table and stared at the laptop computer. His novel — or, more to the point, the absence of his novel — mocked him. What was wrong with him? He never had trouble coming up with his word count as a reporter.

He looked across the room at his jacket. Oh, right — he needed to look something up in his checkbook. He was just working up the energy to go over and look when there was a knock at the door. Who could be pestering him at this hour?

Hunting the living room floor for his clothes, he snatched up his shirt and pants. He yelled, "Just a second!"

He hopped on one leg, then the other, to get his pants on. He had one arm through the sleeve as he squinted out the peephole. The fisheye revealed a small man in a pin-stripe suit wearing a non-regulation fedora. So it wasn't cops or Feds. Or, thank God, the IRS. For some reason, the man had brought a tree with him.

Truman asked through the door, "What do you want?"

"Mr. Truman? Harry Truman?"

"Yes, what is it?"

"Can we speak to you a moment? It involves a lot of money."

"Hold on." Truman was never one to turn down a talk about money. Besides, it wouldn't be the first time a late night visitor showed up at his door with a lead. Truman pushed his other arm through the sleeve and undid the chain. He cracked the door and walked away to finish dressing. "Come on in."

He walked toward the window, still buttoning his shirt. Behind him, he heard the man enter — accompanied by what Truman would later describe as a small earthquake — and close the door. Truman, still preoccupied with his buttons, asked his shirt, "What can I do for you?"

The man cleared his throat. "Are you Harry Truman?"

Truman turned, his grin flickering a bit at the sight of the small man and his large companion. "Yes? What can I do for you?"

"A Mr. Carlin told us we could find you here. We're here to talk about the money."

Truman sighed. This was another Carlin put-on? Where could the man have found this circus act? "Okay, I can spare you a few minutes."

The room was silent as everyone stared at each other. Finally, the little man frowned. He adjusted his tie. "Well? We're waiting."

Truman dropped his grin. "Don't look at me, this is your little presentation. Got a song to go with this routine?"

The little man looked up at the big man. The big man looked down at the little man.

Truman rubbed his hands together. "Look, fellas, whatever this act is, can you get on with it? I'm actually kind of beat."

The little man looked back at Truman. "We're here for our money."

Truman frowned. He looked at the little man. The little man was serious. Truman looked at the big man. The big man was like a shaved bear. The enormous cowboy hat and shiny cowboy boots made him look like a folk legend. Truman cleared his throat. "Um...would it be impolite to ask who you are?"

The little man was still doing all the talking. "We're the guys here to get the money. And we don't care how much we got to stomp on you until we get it."

"I see. And would it be impolite to ask what money I'm supposed to have?"

The little man gave an impatient sigh. "You know very well that we're talking about the half mil."

Truman's eyes got wide. "Wait—what? I never had that. Somebody else was monkeying around with my—"

"Bull Ron." The little man's mouth curved into a sly grin. "This guy is the reason Darla's in trouble."

The shaved bear stooped down to normal-person-size. "Darla?"

The little man nodded. "Right!"

The shaved bear turned and snarled. Truman backed up slowly. "Can we just talk about this?"

The shaved bear grabbed the uncomfortable chair and lifted it over his head. He yelled "Darla!" and threw it at Truman's head.

Truman dodged as the chair whizzed past. "Look, you're making a mistake here!"

"The mistake was yours," the little man said.

The big man now had Truman's TV set up over his head. He yelled "Darla!" again and threw it.

Truman jumped on the couch to avoid the set, which crashed on the floor. "Listen! I never had that money! Somebody else put it in my account and then took it back out!"

"Not good enough," the little man said.

The big man grabbed the card table. It was too flimsy for his purposes, so he threw it against the bookshelf. His eyes scanned the room, searching for some other object to grab. For once, Truman's ridiculously Spartan living room was a lifesaver.

The big man breathed heavily, working himself up into some kind of froth. He glared at Truman up on the couch. The big man charged.

Truman barely had a second to avoid the meaty arms. The springs in the couch helped him jump out of the way.

The enormous man crashed into the wall, his head cracking into plaster. He put both his beefy hands on the wall and pushed until he got his head back. He left an impact crater in the wall.

Truman grabbed his shoes off the floor and pulled on the left one. "Honest! That money was donated to the shelter! I had nothing to do with it!"

Truman was working on the second shoe when the big man charged again and got his fingers around Truman's throat. The big man growled, "Stop hurting Darla!"

Struggling for consciousness, Truman choked out, "You gotta believe me!"

The big man tossed Truman across the room and into the book shelves. Truman fell to the floor amid books and what used to be his card table. He gasped in precious air. He blinked the spots out of his eyes.

Across the room, the big man was readying for another charge. Truman got his back against the wall and pushed himself up. Heart pounding in his ears, he focused on the big man. A flicker of memory returned to him, something he had learned in high school wrestling: He looked at the man's chest. Not his face, not his hands, not his feet. His chest.

The big man, blasting hot breath, eyes blazing, gritting his teeth, charged. Truman waited until the last second and moved to the side. He stuck out his left leg and tripped the big man, who careened into the wooden wall. There was a crash and a thud and a crack, all at once.

The door was blocked by the chair, so Truman raced for the window. He slid it open and stepped out onto the balcony.

The little man yelled, "Hey! Stop!"

Truman looked down over the railing at the ground, three floors down. He looked at the row of bushes below. He looked at the paved parking lot.

He was starting to have second thoughts when he heard the big man brushing off the debris and readying for another charge. Truman stepped over the railing and stood on the thin ledge, positioned himself best he could, shut his eyes and fell two stories into the row of bushes.

He blinked himself back into awareness, surprised that he'd survived the fall. He stood and found his right leg extremely tender, his left ankle wobbly. His face and arms were all scratched up. Otherwise, he seemed relatively unbroken.

Above, his attackers leaned over the railing. The little man pointed. "Hey, you! Get back here!"

Truman turned and began limping across the parking lot. He needed to find a phone. Or a policeman. Or a really large mallet.

He saw his car, but didn't have his keys on him. He'd made the leap with just the clothes on his back — no cell phone, no keys, no wallet, no money, no identification, no nothing. Truman continued limping his way across the parking lot. He thought about banging on the other apartment doors, but that would just get somebody else killed, too. No, he needed the safety of a crowd.

He saw the lights of the one nearby restaurant and made for it. No idea how close the other two men were — they were surely gaining on him — he pushed himself to limp as fast as he could.

At the entrance he pushed inside and headed for the hostess. She made a face at the scruffy, limping intruder. "May I help you?"

Truman leaned on her podium. "Please call the police."

"W-why?"

The door opened and in came the other two men. The little man walked up and asked in a low voice, "Now, we don't want to create a scene, do we?"

That gave Truman an idea. He stumbled his way toward the diners, the woman calling after him, but he made it all the way to the center of the big room. "Ladies and gentlemen, may I have your attention! I have a complaint to level against each and every one of you!"

Most of the diners turned and stared at the interruption. The horrified hostess put a hand on his arm. "Please, sir," she said in an urgent whisper, "if you could just—"

"Oh, no!" Truman shook her off. "You will not silence me! And I will not be silenced short of the police coming here and hauling me off in handcuffs!"

He glanced back and saw the little man and the big man waiting. The little man was scanning the dining room, apparently searching for all the available exits.

Truman, fighting off a wave of dizziness, took a breath and launched into his made-up tirade. "Do you people have any idea how much water that you waste, each and every day? How many gallons of water are polluted every hour? Every minute?"

His mind raced to try and remember the stats that Tina had once told him. At the time, he told her she was crazy. But if he got out of this ordeal alive, once he got out of jail, he owed her a dinner. "Every time you wash your car, every time you buy a bottled water, every time you —"

Truman felt a pinch at the back of his neck and his right arm was suddenly locked in place by a much larger arm. Glancing around, he was relieved to see it was just some guy in white who'd popped out of the kitchen. "All right," the kitchen guy said, "go somewhere else to sleep it off."

"No, wait," Truman struggled. "This is a matter of life and death."

"I know," the kitchen guy replied with a sigh, dragging Truman toward the exit. "It always is with you types."

"You don't understand —"

"Look, you don't really want us to call the police, do you?"

"Yes! Yes, I do!"

"Trust me, you don't," the kitchen guy replied patiently. He got Truman to the door. "When you sober up tomorrow, you'll thank me."

Truman turned back. "Please! You don't understand!"

"Beat it!" The kitchen guy pushed back. Truman

tripped against the curb and fell into the bushes. The man shouted, "And stay out!"

As the man disappeared inside, Truman struggled in the bushes, leaning on his hurt leg, then his hurt ankle, until he got up. The way back inside was blocked by the shaved bear.

The little man put a hand on Truman's shoulder. He said amiably, "We'll be back tomorrow. You'll have the money by then, right?"

TWENTY-ONE

Marion Russell was driving the young hoodlum
Gordon out to a neighborhood out by Brentwood. It
was a good twenty minute drive from downtown,
Marion the whole time congratulating himself on his
brilliance—here he was, on his first mission as an
undercover operative, and he had already insinuated
himself into a criminal gang.

For the first few minutes, there wasn't a lot of
conversation between the two men, just Gordon
offering some directions. But Marion wanted to get a
better handle on the score, in case he needed to call
for backup. Which, of course, would also require
figuring out who and how he would actually call for
backup.

Marion cleared his throat. "So, what can you tell
me about this gig we're on?"

"You're just helping move the stuff."

"Of course, of course." Marion offered his
connection a friendly smile. "I'm hip."

"So it's the usual kind of show. You know—we
set up, knock 'em down, and head out before the
cops show up. Know what I mean?"

"Could get rowdy, huh?"

"If they been drinking. But the chicken wire
protects us from most flying objects."

"Uh-huh, I see what you mean." Of course, he
didn't. Marion wondered whether real undercover
agents went through some kind of orientation before
submersing themselves into the criminal culture like
this. But it was too late now—he was in this thing.
"So, we're headed to the gig now?"

"No, we got to make a stop and pick up the

equipment. Some of the boys should be there to help us load up."

The word "equipment" set Marion's mind on fire. What kind of equipment? Maybe it was tools for breaking into a bank — something to fix the alarm, something to get into the safe, and then whatever it took to transport all the loot. Or it would be for making counterfeit money — engraved plates, ink, paper, presses, that sort of thing. Or maybe they were picking up the components of a meth lab. Or some kind of —

"You know your way around a set of cables, right?"

"Oh, sure, sure," Marion replied, but he wasn't sure at all.

"Because that would be a huge help tonight."

"Like I said, I am here to help." Of course, he was really there to watch and listen and then report whatever he discovered to the authorities. He was starting to feel like Don Johnson.

"Turn here." Gordon pointed at the street sign. They turned down a residential street and went a few blocks before he pointed at a big white house. "Pull into the driveway."

"Shouldn't I park along the street? What if we need to make a quick getaway?"

"Trust me, it goes a lot faster if we're close to the door."

"You're the boss." Marion carefully drove up the long driveway until he reached the big square of blacktop behind the house. Gordon had him back the car up to the porch. The house was completely dark.

At the back door, Marion shivered nervously as he stared up at the big house. Was this the home of some mob kingpin? Or were they about to commit a home invasion against some innocent citizens?

Maybe this was the home of somebody like the District Attorney. Maybe this "equipment" they were getting actually referred to vital evidence in the state's case against organized crime. And Gordon was here to grab it before it could be presented in court.

Whatever foul deed they were here for, Marion was ready to stand for the cause of justice. And once he had the bad guys over a barrel, he could force them to explain Harry Truman's role in their operations. And once Marion got them to testify against that rapscallion—hello promotion. Hello raise. Hello respect from his colleagues and his wife.

All he had to do was survive the night.

"I don't know where Benny is," Gordon said. He rubbed his hands together and glanced around the dark yard. "He should be here."

"Who's Benny?"

"Benny is the guy who gets us inside."

"What do we do now?"

"We may have to do this ourselves. You got a credit card or anything?"

"Um." Marion frowned and reached for his wallet. He pulled it out, hoping that undercover agents got all their expenses reimbursed at the end of a case. "Here."

"Thanks." Gordon opened the screen door and got to work on the door with the credit card. He was trying to jimmy the lock.

Marion glanced at the neighboring houses, trying to calculate from which angles he might be seen. Wondering whether the moonlight was bright enough for witnesses to make out his features. "So once we're in, what's the plan?"

"Just in and out. No muss, no fuss. Right?"

"Right."

There was a sound from inside and the porch light flickered on. A voice from inside demanded, "Who's out there?"

Marion yelled, "Cheese it!" And he ran.

The door opened and a tall blonde in a white bathrobe appeared. "Why, Gordon, is that you?"

"Hi, Mrs. Ritchie. Benny told me to come by and get the instruments for the show tonight. If I knew you were home, I'd have rung the bell."

Mrs. Ritchie heard a loud sneeze out in the yard, and squinted at the figure scrambling over the neighbor's rose bushes. "Who's that?"

"Some guy who offered to help out as our roadie tonight. I guess he flaked out. At least he let me borrow his car."

TWENTY-TWO

Truman's apartment was empty. The living room practically a smoking crater. The old television now a pile of glass and plastic and machine parts. The big chair overturned against the wall. The bookshelves all on the floor, the literary contents now piled like so many stones after an avalanche.

The apartment was still. Empty. Quiet.

Which made the noise all the more remarkable when the battering ram smashed in through the front door. A group of men burst in, all in black with distinctive white lettering announcing them as members of the FBI.

Two men in black trench coats stood at the door. Special Agent Reed asked, "Couldn't we have knocked?"

Special Agent Murphy snarked, "I didn't want him to sneak out the back way."

"What back way? This is an apartment, three stories up. Did you think he'd jump off the balcony into the bushes?"

"Stranger things have happened."

Reed looked at the mess that had been made of the living room. "What did you do?"

Murphy snapped his fingers at the men in the body armor. "Search the place! They have to be here somewhere!"

"What all do we expect to find here?"

"Clues. Money." Murphy shrugged. "The girl."

"You don't have to be this aggressive. We have no cause to even think Truman is involved in this kidnapping business."

"The judge thought we had cause when he

signed the warrant."

"I'm telling you, we need to take another look at Buddy Powell."

"We already discussed your crazy theory. I just don't see it."

"But the ransom money was paid and we still don't have Darla Lovell back. Why doesn't that worry him? Why is he still acting like she's coming back—like he *knows* she's coming back?"

"Maybe he's just got more faith than you."

"It's like he knows where she is and he knows that's she's safe. I mean, why else didn't your little speech freak him out?"

"What speech?"

"That idiotic 'she could be dead already' thing you said. Any normal person would have had a nervous breakdown or punched you in the mouth right then and there."

"Be glad he didn't try that."

"I don't know whether I'd have stopped him."

"I'm putting that in my report."

"It's sure going in mine."

"Let's just keep our eye on the ball here, right? How you fellas doing back there?"

One of the helmeted men popped in from the other room. "We can't find anybody here, sir."

Murphy frowned. "Well, look for hiding places. Don't be afraid to pull out the walls."

"Yes, sir!" The helmeted man took off for the bedroom.

From the back came the sound of more breaking and tossing and crashing and splintering. Reed said, "I guess it could be worse—at least you didn't have to shoot a dog in self-defense."

"Hardy har har." Murphy glanced around nervously. There were no pets this time, right?

Reed picked through the rubble of books. The pile included literary novels, true crime books, and how-to books for playing poker.

Murphy asked, "What do you think happened to Truman?"

"Who knows? Maybe he got a tip we were coming."

"You think so? Because it would be just like that—"

A man burst in the open front door. "All right, Truman, enough is enough! I know what you did, and I am not afraid to tell people!" He stopped and looked at the debris that was the living room. "Wow, what happened here?"

Reed and Murphy shared a look, then Murphy pounced on the man. "Who are you?"

"J-Jack Carlin," the man said, his face going white. "I'm a reporter for the *Nashville View*. What's going on?"

Murphy snapped, "We're the one asking the questions here!"

"We're the FBI," Reed interjected helpfully. "We'd appreciate if you'd answer a couple of questions."

Murphy gripped Carlin's shirt. "Where is Darla Lovell?"

Carlin's eyes went wide. He swallowed air. "How should I know?"

"You said you knew that Truman had kidnapped her—"

"Actually, he didn't say that," Reed corrected. "He said—"

Carlin's eyes went wide. "Wait, are you saying that Truman is the kidnapper?"

"No!" Reed waved his hands. "We did not say that."

Murphy snapped, "We know that Truman has her somewhere, and we know that you're in this up to your neck!"

Reed asked, "How do we know that?"

Carlin went white. "No! Honest! I had no idea until now that Truman kidnapped Darla Lovell!" He licked his lips. "Wait until I get back to the paper."

"Wait," Reed said, "you can't print that. The FBI does not have a suspect at this time."

"Of course we do," Murphy said. "We just have to figure out where Truman is hiding her."

The men in helmets returned from the other parts of the apartment. They had turned the bedroom and the kitchen inside out. "We didn't find anything, sir."

Murphy nodded glumly. "Fine." He turned to Carlin and handed him a card. "If you hear from that low-life, you call me!"

Carlin was giddy. "Of course!"

The FBI left the apartment, Reed just shaking his head. Once they were gone, Carlin went over to the couch and plopped down. He put the FBI man's card in his wallet. While he caught his breath, his eyes scanned the apartment. From his vantage point, he saw into the bedroom. All the overturned bedroom furniture, all the drawers yanked out, their contents strewn about. He turned and looked left into the kitchen. Dishes were smashed on the vinyl floor.

Carlin sat back and laughed. Harry Truman a kidnapper! What a scoop! And, best of all, a chance to show that he, Jack Carlin, was the better reporter after all.

He was still basking in this euphoric state when a large man entered. Carlin remembered him from the man's earlier visit to the newspaper offices.

Carlin smiled. "Hello!"

The large man was craned over, trying to see the carpet from on high.

"Did you lose something?"

"Rabbit's foot. Sherman says I have to find it."

Carlin squinted at the floor, studying the rubble that was the living room. He saw something fuzzy and went over. "Here it is. Anything else?"

"Where is Truman?"

"Why?"

"I got to talk to him."

"What about?"

"I got to talk to him about Darla."

At the sound of the name, Carlin's ears pricked up. He inched closer. "Darla Lovell?"

"Yeh."

"What about her?"

"I got to talk to Truman."

"You got some kind of message for him?"

The large man thought for a second. "Yuh."

"Well, you can give the message to me."

The large man thought for another moment. "I got to talk to Truman."

"But he's not here! Look, you can tell me." Carlin licked his lips, hoping this lead didn't slip through his fingers. He could taste the Pulitzer already. Did the Pulitzer have a taste? "I work with Truman. You could say he and I are partners."

"You work together?"

"Yes, partners! Why is that so hard to understand?" He began tapping a finger on the big man's chest. "We do everything together, you big gorilla! So whatever you got for Truman, give it to me!"

That was the last complete sentence Carlin got out before he woke up again in the hospital some days later. And even after that, he still didn't really talk in complete sentences for a while.

TWENTY-THREE

Marion Russell was on the run—from the law, from organized crime, from anyone and everyone who came to mind. He didn't know who all might be behind him, but his intention was to get away and to get away fast.

In his panic, he had no doubt that the homeowner back there—whether it was the District Attorney, or some mafia kingpin, or even a private citizen—had already alerted their people to chase down the man caught lurking at the back door. Marion wondered how quickly his description would be distributed to every gun owner in the state of Tennessee. Would there be a gang after him? A posse?

Marion raced pell-mell across some eight or ten acres; past fourteen or fifteen mansions; climbed over, burst through, or otherwise damaged a dozen bushes and an equal number of hedges; and snagged and/or ripped his good suit jacket and slacks in several places.

His chest ready to explode, he finally collapsed behind yet another nondescript mansion. Next to a shed beside a swimming pool, he pressed his back against the brick building, hoping to avoid the floodlights that had tripped on as he passed the motion sensors.

Curled up in his hiding place, he gasped for air. Wheezed. Sneezed. Coughed. He'd run as far as he could—he was spent. He just needed to rest a few minutes while he tried to figure out his next move. What does an undercover agent do in this situation? Here he was in enemy territory, his cover blown, with no idea whom he could trust.

The next face he saw might be the face of a killer. Carrying a gun. With a bullet. With his name on it.

Marion wished more than ever that he'd taken some kind of orientation course before embarking on this mission. He should have known it wouldn't be easy trying to catch a mastermind like Truman.

He needed to find a way to get in touch with the authorities. Since he had never actually cleared this undercover operation with any government agency — not the FBI, not the CIA, not even his bosses at the IRS — Marion wasn't sure whom to contact in this situation. Maybe he should just start with the local police. He wished he was carrying his cell phone, but he had lost it along with his wallet and his keys and, oh, yeah, his car.

"Who's back there?" A shadow appeared over him. "You all right?"

Marion sneezed. "I'm fine."

"Can I ask what you're doing in my backyard?"

Marion struggled to stand. If this was a killer, the man was playing it cool. But Marion could play it cool, too. "I was just passing through."

"Hey, are you bleeding? Maybe you better come inside where we can look at those scratches."

Marion decided his best chance was to play along until he could get to a telephone. "Sure."

They headed for the house. The man asked, "Are you lost?"

"Yeah. I'm from out of town, and I got turned around in the dark."

"If you're all the way out here, you must have got turned around pretty bad."

In the light of the porch, the man didn't look like

a killer. (But did they ever? Now, see, this is the sort of thing one might have learned at an orientation.)

They entered the house through a large kitchen. With the bright lights and warm earth tones and the smell of freshly brewed coffee, Marion found his muscles starting to relax. In this environment, the elderly man seemed less threatening than ever—he was in his seventies, but fit, charming, pleasant, with a thin wisp of white hair circling the bald crown on his head. He was wrapped in a comfortable brown terry cloth robe, and wearing fluffy slippers.

The man led Marion to the kitchen table. "You sit down while I get out some disinfectant and bandages. You need some coffee? I just made some. But I'm afraid it's decaf."

Marion forced a smile. "That sounds great."

The man poured Marion a cup and set it on the table, then disappeared from the kitchen. Marion cupped both hands around the warm mug, feeling the tingle in his fingers. He allowed the aroma of the coffee to revive him, and then took in a series of long slurps. Even without caffeine, the rich, warm liquid gave him a jolt. It was like he'd been yanked back from the precipice, and now his blood was pumping with a surge of life and gratefulness and whatever else you feel after being yanked back from a precipice. It was good.

He glanced across the kitchen and saw a telephone on the wall. He still needed to call the police—if only to check in. He set down the cup and forced his weary muscles to carry him over there.

Marion picked up the receiver and heard the old man's voice. "He's right here," the old man was saying. "I'm telling you, this will be easier than I ever imagined."

Another voice asked, "Can you get him over there tonight?"

The old man replied, "As soon as I bandage him up, I'll get to work on him."

TWENTY-FOUR

It was sometime after midnight when Truman arrived at the home of Jack Carlin. Following his altercation with the ox that walked like a man, and the threat made by the short man who appeared to be the ox's handler, Truman was not about to stay at home. He had rushed through the apartment and grabbed whatever he could carry, just jammed a couple bags full of random clothes and toiletries. He hadn't bothered to take the cell phone — until he paid the bill, it was just dead weight.

Truman parked at the curb. The neighborhood appeared to be locked down for the night. Limping on a hurt leg and a twisted ankle, he lugged the bags of wadded clothing and toiletries up to the porch. He had never actually been here before, but knew the address from his days snooping through personnel files at the newspaper.

Back when he dug up Carlin's address, it seemed like an awfully upscale neighborhood for a man who worked for a living. Clearly, Carlin was getting his money from somewhere else.

The house was dark and there were no cars around. Certain that Carlin was still out at the lake, Truman cast a careful glance toward the street, then limped around back. A set of lights flicked on automatically, flooding the backyard with light.

At the patio doors, he set down his bags and got to work on the lock. It took a matter of seconds to get inside and disarm the home security system. You don't spend your career asking questions of professional criminals without picking up a few tips.

He felt a gurgle in his stomach and wondered

whether it was rage or an ulcer. Or maybe the former was creating the latter.

All his bruises, the fracture to his manhood and self-esteem, the damages to his apartment — even the fact that Truman was now afraid to sleep in his own home — that was all the fault of Jack Carlin. As such, it was only right that Jack Carlin had a houseguest until this all blew over. Whether Truman was the Oscar or the Felix was up to Carlin.

Inside, he closed the blinds and stumbled around for a light switch. He found a lamp — caught it before he knocked it off the end table, actually — and felt under the lampshade until he found the switch.

Truman was shocked at the ugliness of the room. Velvet paintings on the wall, wall-to-wall purple shag carpeting, and the lamps were all shaped like fountain statues. All the striped furniture pointed toward an enormous flat screen television, which itself was surrounded by an obnoxious variety of electronic equipment.

At the white couch, he dropped his bags, kicked off his shoes, and pulled off his socks. Now that he lived here, he might as well make himself comfortable. He stood and wrinkled his toes in the thick carpeting. It was ugly but it was soft.

He wandered through the hall to see where it led. He stumbled on his ankle, and got fingerprints on the wall. He looked at his hands — they were filthy.

Reaching a bedroom, he flipped on the light, bracing himself for a quick explanation if he woke up Carlin. But the bed was empty. Yep, Carlin must be at the lake.

Truman shuffled, bare feet still luxuriating in the shag carpet, over to the bed. He stepped up onto the bed and jumped up and down a few times. It felt firm. Good.

His next stop was the enormous white kitchen. He padded across the kitchen floor—the cold linoleum was not nearly as pleasant as the shag carpet—and flipped on the light. At the sink, he turned on the faucet and held a hand under the water until it turned warm. The bar of soap turned black as he lathered up. He rinsed his hands and turned off the water, and yanked a white linen towel off the rack. The towel also turned black.

He tossed the damp towel on the counter. He didn't know whether his new roommate was a stickler for putting things back—they'd have to discuss that when they divvied up their chores. It was only fair that each roommate did his part.

He went through the cabinets and drawers. Pots and pans. A lot of dishes and glassware with a matching flowery pattern. More silverware than a bachelor had any business owning. Of course, now that the house was occupied by two bachelors, the ratio was a little more acceptable.

The pantry was full of beef jerky and foreign coffee. And a lot of knickknacks that apparently had been shoved in here in lieu of a junk drawer.

The fridge, however, was more like it: Various kinds of cheeses, lunchmeat, and bagels. A big jug of sangria. The freezer contained pizzas and waffles and chicken tenders.

Truman's stomach growled again. He pulled out a pizza. It took him a few minutes to figure out how to work the oven. Eventually, he switched it on and, without waiting to preheat, tore the plastic wrap off the pizza and set it on the grill.

The sangria had a twist top, so he grabbed it and headed for the living room. Too weary to worry about a glass, he just twisted off the top and drank right out of the bottle.

He plopped down on the white couch, and propped up his feet on the armrest. He took a swig of the sangria, and let out a big sigh of relief. It was like he had been holding his breath all night. Maybe not literally, but certainly figuratively. Lying on this white couch, bare feet making prints on the white material—apparently, he needed to wash his feet, too—he chugged sangria, the sweet, red liquid running all over his mouth and down his face.

Ahhh.

He shut his eyes and let the calmness wash over him. No worries. Just ignore the aching in his limbs. Forget about the bad men trying to kill him. His apartment being trashed. This thing with his bank account. The mysterious IRS agent. The FBI buzzing about him. About his money troubles, his book troubles, his employment troubles.

He let his imagination take him to a happy place. A beach. The sun warming his face. The ocean lapping against the warm sand. Palm trees. Scantily clad island women, all ready to—

Where was that beeping coming from? There was no beeping on the beach. Somebody's alarm, or maybe cell phone, or possibly—

Ah. Smoke alarm.

The pizza.

Truman bolted upright, dropping the sangria on the couch. He jumped up and ran for the kitchen.

Fighting his way through smoke, he threw open some windows, grabbed some potholders, and yanked the pizza out of the oven.

He was too late to save this particular pizza, so he threw it in the sink. He went to the freezer, unwrapped another pizza, and tried again.

***

A half hour later, full of pizza and sangria, Truman tried to figure out where the guest room was. He couldn't find one, so he went back to what must have been Carlin's room. He stripped to his underwear, dropped his clothes on the carpet, fell into the bed, and pulled the blankets up tight.

He was a light sleeper, so he expected to hear when Carlin got home. Truman wondered how long the moron would stick it out at the lake.

As he drifted toward sleep, a question lurked at the edges of his consciousness. Those men tonight, the ones who beat him up—what exactly was their relationship to the money? And why did they think he still had it?

Then he was asleep.

TWENTY-FIVE

Marion Russell had to find a weapon. He was too exhausted to run—not to mention, he had no idea where he would go—so his only hope for survival was to make a stand right here in this stranger's house.

He began digging through the kitchen drawers. A junk drawer had an assortment of useless odds and ends, batteries and light bulbs and cards and paperclips and bolts and rubber bands. Another drawer had kitchen utensils—spatulas and various measuring devices and other things—none of which seemed practical in fending off a killer.

He found the silverware drawer, and even held a big knife in his hand—but he didn't think he had the stomach to use it effectively. The cabinets just held plates and glasses and crockware.

He moved to the pantry. Just shelves of cans and dried goods. On the wall were pegs on which hung cloth towels and potholders.

What he really needed was something big he could swing—a baseball bat or a golf club, something like that. But the man didn't keep those here in the pantry. Here was a broom, but the handle was too flimsy for combat.

In the hall, Marion pulled open the drawers in a credenza. Photo albums. Stacks of papers.

He glanced in the side room and saw a black object under a bed. A gun! He leaped into the room, threw himself to the floor, and stretched for it. He held the lump of death in his hand, trying to become acquainted with it. He needed to familiarize himself with it if he was going to—

The other man was coming back. Marion would have to bluff his way through this. He really, really wished he'd taken that orientation. He didn't know whether they really had that sort of thing, but it sure seemed like a good idea right now.

So Marion scrambled for the best spot in the kitchen — he ended up with his back in the corner, between the refrigerator and the counter. To his right was the sink and the garbage disposal. To his left was the fridge, and then cabinets. All the windows, doors, and other visible entrances were all in front of him. There was no way somebody could sneak up behind him.

The old man was whistling as he entered the kitchen. He stopped when he saw that his quarry had moved from the chair.

Marion held up the weapon in his best TV cop pose. "Hold it right there!"

"What's all this now?" The man slowly began slipping his hands in the pockets of his fluffy robe.

"Hands where I can see them! I know how to use this!" Of course, Marion had no idea how to fire a gun, but he hoped the man didn't notice the trembling hands. Or hear the crack in his voice.

The old man put up his hands. "I'd appreciate if you told me what this is about."

"I heard you on the phone."

"I don't know what you think you heard—"

"I heard enough. I know exactly who you are."

"You do?"

"Some mob killer sent to rub me out."

"Huh?" The old man cocked an eyebrow. "You were in my backyard. You were sent to me."

Marion had to stop and think about this. What

the man said seemed reasonable—but then, that's what a mob killer would want him to think. Maybe the old man was just trying to lull his victim into a false sense of security. I mean, who would suspect a killer to be wearing those fluffy slippers? No, the disguise was too perfect not to be a disguise.

Marion braced one arm with the other to hold the gun steady. "Nice try."

"I think you're woozy from loss of blood, son. We still need to take a look at those scratches. You don't want to get tetanus."

"Just hold it right there. Hands up."

"So I'm just supposed to hold this pose for the rest of the night?"

"No, just until—" Marion stopped. He'd never called the police. He was alone in this house with this man and was backed into this corner. He was trapped. "I'm going to go over to the phone. Back away slowly—and remember that I've got this."

He inched forward, the old man watching. He stumbled, and the man went to catch him.

Marion pulled the trigger.

TWENTY-SIX

The next morning, Buddy Powell and Wanda Lovell were in the car headed for Waterdale Homes. Momma Lovell had her window down, dangling her cigarette out the open passenger window. She tapped the cigarette, and the ashes flew in the wind. "How many days it been now?"

Buddy looked over, a hand on the steering wheel and an elbow out the window. "Since what?"

"Since my baby been home."

"I don't know, hon. A couple weeks."

"Seems longer than that."

He put a hand on her knee. "It'll be over soon. And we'll give Darla the biggest homecoming any country star ever got! I'm thinking an entire tour— the cities to be determined by which radio stations get on board with our whole yellow ribbon campaign."

"It's gonna be a big tour?"

"The biggest! And it will culminate in a whole celebration when we get back here to Nashville. We're negotiating broadcast rights even as we speak." He laughed. "Once we get to the end of this campaign, there won't be a country music fan in the world who don't know the name 'Darla Lovell.'"

"That sounds fine." Wanda took another drag on her cigarette. "You sure this is all gonna work out?"

"How could it not work out? Hon, we got it all in the palm of our hands. I been making the calls from the office—"

"With them government agents out there?"

"What difference does that make? Ain't no harm in making some calls to promote Darla's career. They expect it."

"So how do we explain the fact that Darla ain't back yet?"

"We don't gotta explain nothin'."

"I thought we were still waiting on the money."

"It'll get sorted out. And then we can bring Darla home."

"So why don't your kidnappers just send another ransom note?"

Buddy looked over and grimaced. "The insurance company won't send any more money than they did. Are you willing to put in your own money?"

She shrugged. "If we're keeping it all in the family."

"Yeah, but what if something goes wrong with that drop and we lose that money, too?"

"Oh. Then no."

"Besides, if we pay the ransom ourselves, we hardly get a buck out of this, do we?"

"I guess not."

They drove on a bit in silence. They passed pockets of developed land alternating with undeveloped land—so, rows of strip malls and gas stations and antique shops, followed by stretches of tall grass and farmland and grazing livestock.

Wanda asked, "So, where'd the ransom money go?"

"Somebody stole it."

"That's funny."

"I ain't laughing." Buddy snorted. "But we're gonna find it. Don't you worry."

They got to the house at Waterdale and Buddy pulled into the steep driveway. "Now, I wanna warn you, it may not look pretty in there. But until your daughter gets her head on straight, we got to make sure she don't talk to the wrong people. Know what I mean?"

"Sometimes that girl gets bull-headed. Just like her no-good father."

Inside the house, the upstairs was quiet as death. Wanda asked, "So, what do you want me to tell Darla?"

"Just make it clear to her that this was a kidnapping, fair and square. She don't know who those boys are, she don't know where she was, she don't know nothing but she was gone and she'll be glad to get home to her momma."

"What's so hard about that?"

"Exactly my point. But your daughter has got it in her head to always tell the truth. Ain't no profit in that. And better she learn it now than later."

"Heh." Wanda took another long drag from her cigarette and glanced around. "Where are the boys?"

"In the process of getting our money back."

She didn't see an ashtray, so she went to the kitchen and dug in the cabinets for a saucer. She set it on the counter and tapped her cigarette ashes onto it.

Buddy asked, "So, you know what to say to her?"

"Uh-huh. So, where is my Darla?"

"We had to lock her up in the studio."

"Poor thing."

"We can't risk her running out and talking to the neighbors. Not until we get some things straight. And definitely not before we get that money." He huffed in disgust. "Who ever heard of kidnappers that returned a body before they got the money?"

"Well, she's not really kidnapped."

"It's the principle of the thing." He led her out of the kitchen and across the living room. They reached the door to the stairs, the one with the padlock. He grabbed the key off the end table, unlocked the padlock, undid the latch, and opened the door. He stepped back to allow ladies first.

Wanda stood at the top of the stairs. Smoking. Staring down at the blackness. Taking the steps in her platform shoes, she carefully negotiated her way down. About halfway, she stopped and bent to look at something. "What are all these on the steps? Little dolls or something."

Buddy, behind her, couldn't see what she was talking about. "I got no idea. Keep a going."

At the bottom, Wanda coughed. "Darla, hon? You down here?"

A voice squeaked, "I'm over here, Momma."

Wanda found her daughter huddled in the corner of the room. All these fine couches and chairs down here, and her daughter was curled up in the corner like a dog. The things that got in that girl's head.

"C'mon, baby, get up." Wanda reached down and took her daughter's hand, and led Darla over to one of the couches. "There, that's better. How you been, baby? I missed you."

"You here to take me home?"

"Not yet, hon."

Darla glanced in the direction of Buddy, standing silently to the side. Then she looked at her momma. "They're keeping me locked up down here."

"I know, hon, but it's important. You wanna be a

star, don'tcha? Well, every country music star had to go through their little trials before they became famous."

The little girl made a face. Was she gonna cry?

"Here, here, hon." Wanda brushed Darla's hair out of her eyes. "As long as you're away, that gives folks a chance to miss you. And then when this is all over, your fans will surely be glad to see you home."

Buddy chimed in, "That's right."

Wanda said, "Your Uncle Buddy has got a whole, big homecoming planned for you. Ain't that right, Buddy?"

"Absolutely," he agreed. "Big name celebrities, a big tour, all the flowers and ribbons a girl could ever want. You'll be like a princess on one of them there parade floats. By the time we're done, there won't be a music buyer in the world who don't have you on their iPod."

"I don't wanna be a singer no more."

Wanda smacked her girl on the side of the head. "Now, what kinda attitude is that? If the good Lord gives you a gift, it's a sin to let it go to waste."

Darla scrunched up her face. "The Lord didn't tell them to keep me locked up down here."

"Well, hon, it's like that time where they put the man in the lion's cave. Remember that from Sunday school? They put the man in the lion's cave, and then they missed him, and then when he came out he was famous throughout all the land. That's what we're doing here, baby."

"That's not the story."

"You don't talk back to your mother! I think I know the story of the man in the lion's cave." She brushed a hand across her daughter's hair again.

"When can I go home?"

"Soon, baby. Now, Uncle Buddy is keeping you down here for your own protection. Ain't that right, Buddy?"

The man cleared his throat. "That is surely right."

Wanda touched her daughter's cheek. "See, baby? We're doing all this for you. Now, when it's safe to come out again, you just need to remember to tell all them that you don't know who kidnapped you. They were strangers. Right? And you just leave Uncle Buddy and them boys out of it."

"But that'd be lying. You always told me to never tell a lie."

"This isn't a lie, baby. This is…this is…" She turned to Buddy. "What do you call this?"

"A creative solution."

"Yeah, baby, a 'creative solution.'"

"What does that mean?"

"It's grown-up stuff, baby. Just you keep safe down here, and when you get out, just keep your mouth shut and let your momma do all the talking. Understand?"

Darla just sat there. She was staring into nothing. Her eyes were red, but apparently she was all cried out.

Wanda made like everything was square. "There, that's settled. So you be good, and I'll see you again soon."

"You'll come back to see me?"

"Well, I got a lot on my plate, baby. But we'll see."

Upstairs again, Wanda watched Buddy replace the padlock on the door to the stairs. She lit up another cigarette and took a puff. "So, whaddaya think?"

"I don't know. You think she'll do right by us?"

"What if we tell folks she was hypnotized? Her kidnappers did some kinda voodoo on her and made her confused about what really happened?"

Buddy grunted. "Maybe. But who know what'll happen if some police hypnotist puts her under for real and starts poking around?"

"Well, what if we run off for Canada?"

Buddy raised an eyebrow. "What, you and me?"

"And we take Darla. Hide her out in the mountains out there—they got mountains in Canada, right?—until she gets a chance to figure things out. Maybe the change of scenery will do us all some good."

"Not far enough. Besides, if the mountains were gonna do it, we have plenty of those around here."

"How about Europe? Cruise ship or a castle or something?"

"We'd never get her out of the country. The FBI has probably got all the country's exits locked up tighter than...than—what's something that's real tight?"

Wanda took a drag on her cigarette and shrugged. "Don't know."

"Well, at any rate, real tight. Ain't no way we're getting that little girl of yours out of the country before this all blows over."

"I can't believe you got us into this without discussing it with Darla first."

"Who knew she wouldn't get with the program? I thought you raised a smarter girl than that."

"So, what happens if Darla never gets with your

program?"

"I don't know." Of course, Buddy did. He just did not know how Momma Lovell would deal with it. If the time came, would he need one bullet or two?

TWENTY-SEVEN

Late morning, the sun streamed through open curtains into the bedroom. Truman slowly became aware of his sore limbs. He lifted his head and squinted at his surroundings. His head hurt, but it didn't feel like a hangover. He just hurt. As the fog cleared in his head, he took note that he had more aches and pains than he knew he had body parts.

And then it all slowly came back to him.

Ah. Of course. The money. The thugs. The drop from the balcony. The restaurant.

Carlin.

At the thought of the name, the rage and/or ulcer fired up. He sat up and thought the name again.

Carlin.

Which brought up a variety of questions at this juncture. It was late morning, and Truman had woken up in the bed of his own accord—not by an angry homeowner, not by the police, not by anyone.

Surely, Carlin wasn't still conducting his lakeside vigil. Even if the sucker still believed there was supposed to be a drug deal, surely even he wasn't stupid enough to think it would happen in broad daylight.

Oh, well. Truman even shrugged to the empty room. Maybe Carlin got all tuckered out and fell asleep under a bush or something. He'd be awake again soon enough. All it took was one dog to, well, mark said bush and Carlin would be right up. No point worrying about Carlin right now.

Truman's stomach gurgled again. He realized it could also indicate he was starving. Time for breakfast.

He threw back the covers and was shocked at all the bruises lining his body. He rolled out of the bed and tested his leg and his ankle. His toes enjoyed getting reacquainted with the shag carpeting. Ah.

Truman yawned. Truman stretched. Truman scratched himself in places.

Naked, he padded into the kitchen, wondering indifferently whether that sort of thing bothered Carlin. Now that they were housemates, that's the kind of stuff they'd have to work out: Schedules for nudity in the house. For using the water. Washing dishes. Vacuuming. Etc.

Not that Truman was really a schedule-follower. His second wife, bless her heart, was very conscious of schedules. Leila very nearly tolerated the random hours his work required. However, she simply would not stand for his refusal to not shower simply because he felt dirty.

After, say, a stakeout in a Kentucky swamp, taking copious notes while he witnessed the illegal transfer of bootleg livestock, the whole night up to his knees in filthy water in which the livestock would relieve themselves, he'd get home afterward and really feel the need for a shower.

But, of course, it wasn't on the schedule. She had it all in the spreadsheet—to Leila, a shower wasn't simply a shower: it was the use of the water; it was the electricity for the hot water; it was the electricity, and the water, and the detergent to later clean the towels. It was a whole thing.

So, of course, it didn't matter that he came in smelling like cow flop. When you use the shower off-schedule, the terrorists win.

Truman hoped Carlin wouldn't turn out to be like Leila. Otherwise, Carlin would have to leave.

So the naked houseguest was in the fridge again, pulling out everything that looked good for breakfast. He stuck a carton of eggs under one arm, bacon and sausage under the other, and grabbed the carton of milk.

At the stove, he grabbed a flowery bowl out of the cabinet and cracked all dozen eggs into it. He dug out some skillets and soon had bacon crackling in one and ground sausage crackling in the other. The hot grease spat on his bare chest a couple times, reminding him why he rarely cooked bacon naked. He went through the cabinets until he found an apron with a picture of a barbeque grill on it.

Nearly covered by the apron, he stirred the raw egg yolks with a fork, poured in some milk and stirred some more. He grabbed the loaf of bread and stopped. When making French toast, do you put the slices of bread first in a toaster? Or is the "toast" part the thing you do in the skillet? Well, with a whole loaf of bread here, and a whole carton of eggs there, he had enough raw material to experiment.

***

Once the sink was full of skillets and pots and pans and bowls, he took all the food down the hall to the den. The coffee table was barely large enough to hold the entire spread: A giant stack of French toast in several varieties; bacon cooked to various stages of crispness; sausage crumbles piled in a big bowl; a pitcher each of orange juice and milk, and what was left of the sangria. It was more than he personally expected to eat or drink, but who knew whether Carlin or the police might show up for breakfast.

He sat his naked butt on the white couch, and flopped his bare feet on the coffee table. He chomped eagerly on sandwiches made out of French toast and bacon. The sausage sandwich didn't work as well — the greasy crumbs kept falling out on the couch.

He generally liked to read with his breakfast, but there was no evidence that Carlin had any reading material whatsoever. No newspapers, no magazines, no books. Which, of course, seemed odd for a man who was supposed to be making his living with words.

Truman grabbed the remote and tried to figure out the giant TV. His fingers were greasy, so it took a few tries to work his way around the buttons on the remote.

One button turned on the stereo system. Another the CD player, which apparently held multiple discs. Truman clicked through, checking on the sort of music his host considered worthy. Disc 1: Hair metal band from the 1980s. Disc 2: Same. Disc 3: Same.

In fact, there were thirty discs in the changer altogether — and the vast majority of them were bands from the 1980s. Of the discs that did not fall into this category, one was a classical music CD; one was an old country music CD; and one was a sound effects CD that just played the sounds of the ocean.

He chose the country music CD — the greatest hits of Trick Henderson — and pressed his thumb on the volume button to test out the sound system. It got loud. The rhythm section of "Wives and Other Mistakes" chugged along like an old freight train, at this volume rattling the dishes on the coffee table.

He scratched his butt and leaned back on the white couch, basking in the loud music. He could never listen to music at this level back at the apartment.

Wondering about the neighbors, he got his butt off the couch and padded over to the patio doors. He opened the blinds to let in the sunshine, then opened the doors to let in the cool morning air.

Standing there behind the small apron, Truman gazed across an enormous and immaculate green lawn. Why in the world didn't Carlin have a swimming pool?

A series of bushes dotted the property line between this yard and the neighbors on either side. The bushes were short and spaced apart so they didn't really create any privacy. There was a shed at the far end.

Next door, an older person in short sleeves and short pants and red socks and a visor and enormous dark glasses carried a set of short clippers across his/her yard. The person, who began pruning a short tree, glanced in Truman's direction and gave a halting wave.

Truman, glad he was behind at least the apron, gave a hearty wave back. He left the door open — the fresh breeze made a nice counterpoint to the smell of grease and burned bacon wafting through the house — and headed back for the couch. He thought about gathering up all the dishes off the coffee table, but then stopped himself.

Pfft. Later.

Truman went to the den and dug through his wrinkled grocery bags for some clothing. He poured the contents out on the white couch and sifted through what he brought. Apparently, no fresh underpants.

He headed back to the bedroom. Surely, Carlin had some he could borrow.

TWENTY-EIGHT

The bright light called to Marion Russell. He squinted at sunlight streaming in through sheer curtains in front of big picture windows.

What happened? His brain was cloudy, his thinking like cotton candy that had been left to dissolve on the curb. The last thing he remembered was shooting the old man.

And then everything had gone black. Had somebody clobbered him from behind? How was that possible?

More to the point—was he alive? He shut his eyes and took a quick inventory: Head pounding. Mouth dry. Throat sore. Breathing difficult.

Where was he now? With some effort he opened his eyes again, managing tiny slits, lifted his head, and twisted to see his surroundings.

He appeared to be in a spacious living room. The walls were a brilliant yellow, and the room was filled with glowing white furniture. With this headache, Marion did not want to see any brilliant yellow or glowing white right now.

He was on a couch. The couch was large. The pattern on it was a series of exotic birds. The couch was covered in plastic.

Marion sat up with a jolt. Why was he lying on plastic? Was it to protect the couch from his blood? Had he been shot or stabbed or bludgeoned?

Heart pounding in his ears, he patted himself best he could, looking for any holes created in his body. He appeared to be intact. He did not appear to be bleeding. Even the scratches were caked over with dried blood.

He lay back down and closed his eyes. He tried to slow his breathing, wishing his heart would stop making such a racket.

A voice floated from across the room. "Good, you're awake. I was worried there might be some permanent damage."

With herculean effort, Marion opened his eyes and glanced over. The old man had entered, still wearing his fuzzy house robe and fuzzy slippers. Marion tried to answer, but all that came out of his mouth was a gurgle.

"Here, let me get you something to drink." The man disappeared from the living room. There was a clatter from the next room—presumably the kitchen—and then he reappeared with a glass of clear liquid. "Here, this will make you feel better."

Marion struggled to sit up. With a trembling hand he accepted the glass and took a gulp. He saw lightning. He coughed.

The old man laughed. "That moonshine is the best thing for waking up! Any man who isn't glad to be alive after that is dead!"

Marion closed his eyes and waited for the stars to pass. He croaked, "Water?"

"Oh, you want some of that, too?" The man sounded disappointed. He went out of the room again and returned with an identical glass, also filled with a clear liquid.

Marion sniffed the second glass. He sniffed the first glass. He blinked, and sniffed the second glass again. Sipped just a little bit. Once he was relatively certain the beverage was not going to attack him, he gulped it down. It wasn't cold, but he didn't care.

The old man sat across from him in the armchair.

"Got quite a shock there, didn't you?"

"What happened?"

"You had it turned backward."

Marion looked down at his belly. "I shot myself? B-but how—"

"Shot?" The old man laughed. "Son, that was a taser you got hold of. I tried to get it before you zapped yourself, but then—well, here you are."

"Shouldn't you have taken me to a hospital or something?"

"To be frank, you were a stranger in my house, and spouting off a lot of weird stuff. I wasn't quite sure what to do with you. I didn't want to give the authorities an opportunity to poke around here. Folks claim to be open-minded, but a religious man can still face persecution."

"So, am I free to leave?"

"What's your name, son?"

Marion hesitated. "Marion."

"Good to meet you, Marion. I'm Arlen Stone."

"Hello, Arlen."

"So, let me ask you this, Marion." The old man tilted his head. "Where would you go?"

Marion wasn't sure how to answer that. For a few minutes, he'd forgotten he was a fugitive—but now the horrible truth was all rushing back to him. He was a wanted man stuck behind enemy lines. And as long as nobody knew he was here...

"In a sense," the old man was saying, "we are all travelers who have lost our way. We're all far from home."

"How did you know I was from out of town?"

"You said that last night."

"Oh. Right. So, if you're not going to kill me—

and, for the sake of argument, let's say that you're not — then what was all that about on the phone? You were talking about me, right?"

The man hesitated. Then he sat forward in the chair and looked right into Marion's soul. "I was talking with my brothers about offering you a chance to escape."

"Escape?"

"A chance for a new life."

"New life?"

The old man nodded, his eyes twinkling. "You can shed the cares of this world and embrace the warmth of the next. How does that sound to you, Marion?"

"I don't know —"

"We could whisk you away from all this, Marion. Take you somewhere far from the city, for a chance to have some solitude. Peace. Quiet. Someplace where no one knows where you are. No one can bother you."

Marion only heard the part about being able to hide from the law and from the mob. "Where is this place?"

"Not far from here. Our — *church* — has a private resort in the hills."

Marion licked his chapped lips. "How soon can we go?"

The man shot up from the chair. "Just a second."

As the man left the room, Marion felt hope rising in his chest. He didn't know what religion these folks were into, but if they had some kind of monastery where he could hide out until this all blew over, he could surely survive a few hymns and maybe some chanting. How bad could it be?

The man returned with a hooded robe, and tossed it to Marion. "You'll need this."

TWENTY-NINE

Out at the house in Waterdale, Sherman Clayton and Bull Ron were in the upstairs kitchen. Bull Ron had his beefy hands clasped on the table. "Can't we just let her upstairs?"

The smaller man was eating a sandwich. "Can't risk anyone seeing her. Even with the scarf and glasses. You don't know the caterwauling I got that time we took her to the grocery store."

"Just ain't right, keeping a nice girl like that down there. Like we got her in prison or something."

"Look, I understand exactly where you're coming from. But we are in a tight spot here."

Bull Ron snorted. "So, whut are you saying?"

"All Darla's troubles are on account of this Truman fella. If you really want to help her, all we gotta do is get that ransom money from him. Then your little friend will be let go, all safe and sound."

"So, why aren't we hanging around waiting for this guy to get home?"

"Because now that the Feds were there, he ain't gonna go back anytime soon. I should never have let him out of our sight."

"Huh."

"I guess we need to go back to the mission there and see if we can find those homeless guys that double-crossed us. Maybe they'll tell us where he is."

"We get this guy, and Darla will be okay?"

"Absolutely." Clayton was probably lying, but he figured it better to placate the big animal. Besides, he had more important stuff to worry about. He felt in his jacket pocket for the coin. "I got to go do some business. Can I trust you to stay here and keep things under control?"

Bull Ron furrowed his brow. "Control what?"

Clayton sighed. "I'm asking if you can just keep cool?"

"Whut would—"

"Just stay here and don't do anything. Right?"

"Right."

The small man left for his mysterious errand. Bull Ron went to the front room and looked out the big picture window. He watched Clayton get in the car and drive away.

Once it was safe, he went to the living room and grabbed the fancy checker set. A couple pieces tumbled off and fell to the carpet. He took a step and heard a crunch. Holding the board with one hand, he grabbed the key and undid the padlock. Another figurine fell off the game board and onto the carpet. He set the padlock, the key still in it, back on the table.

The trip downstairs was a tight fit—he had to watch his head, plus trying to balance a big stone board covered with loose carved figures. By the time he got to the bottom, there were more pieces on the floor than on the board.

At the bottom, he looked around for Darla. She was across the den, sitting on the couch. He held up the board and grinned triumphantly. "Got a game for you."

She looked at him vacantly. She had her arms wrapped around her, her knees pulled up tight, bare feet on the edge of the couch. "I'm not in the mood to play checkers."

His grin fell. He glanced around the den. There were emptied, sloppy boxes of food all over. He stood at the base of the stairs, unsure where to set down the game. Finally, he stomped across to the kitchenette and set it on the stove. He turned, wiping his hands together like he'd done a hard task.

She asked, "Can I just go home?"

"No, ma'am." He sat on the couch next to her. He sighed like a massive animal heaving out hot breath. "Not yet."

They sat on the couch, staring at the steps that led up to the house. She reached out and put her hand on top of his. She cried.

When the sobbing subsided, he handed her his rabbit's foot. "Here."

She sniffled and laughed. "Thanks."

"How's your food holding out?"

"I think I ate everything I could find. Not much else to do down here."

"You could sing in the studio there."

"I don't feel like singing anymore."

After they were silent again for a time, he started to get up. She asked, "Can you just stay a little longer?"

THIRTY

Truman didn't see a problem exploring Carlin's bedroom closet—roommates share clothes all the time. He pulled out a few hangers' worth of shirts and slacks and threw them on the bed for inspection.

He noticed a cordless phone on the nightstand. He picked it up, clicked it on, and listened to the dial tone. He clicked it off and set it back. He wondered what kind of range something like this had. Would it work in any room of the house? Out in the yard? At the neighbors?

Also on the nightstand was a small flyer. Apparently, a local grocer delivered. Scribbled in the margin were the words "On account."

Truman clicked on the cordless phone and dialed the number. "Hello, I see here that you deliver? Do you have an account for Jack Carlin? Good—I'd like to place an order and put it on his account. Let's see...do you have toasted ravioli? Too bad. All right then, bring some canned ravioli. Better make it a case. Oh, and a loaf of bread, and a dozen eggs. And some milk. And some orange juice. And some frozen pizzas—just throw in an assortment.

"Do you have a cheese department? Got any of those big wheels of cheese? I don't really care what flavor, as long as it's the biggest wheel you got.

"How about ribs—you got barbecued ribs cooked and ready to eat? Add a tub of slaw, a tub of baked beans, and one of those big bags of frozen steak fries.

"You got beer? Throw in a case of every type you got. Right, every type. Right, all on the account of Jack Carlin.

"Oh, wait—you got any magazines or newspapers there? Bring us one copy of every magazine and every newspaper you carry. Yes, all of them. Got any books? Right, one copy of each. Just put it all on the account.

"Got that? Wow, that all adds up, doesn't it? See you when you get here."

He clicked off the phone, and looked at the clothes stretched out on the bed. He felt like getting washed up before trying on anything. The man on the phone said he had a half hour before the delivery would show up—plenty of time for a quick shower.

In the bathroom, there were towels in the linen closet. He found a bar of soap and a bottle of shampoo and turned on the water. He tested the flow with his hand, adjusting the temperature until it was just hot enough.

The hot water felt great on his sore muscles. He was all lathered up when he heard a loud clanging. Was that the doorbell? He switched off the water, grabbed the towel and wiped the soap out of his eyes. He twirled the towel on top of his head into a turban. He grabbed a fluffy robe off the hook and slipped it on.

Dripping on the carpet as he walked through the house, he got turned around in the hall. The bell tolled again before he found his way to the front door. He opened the door, but it wasn't his delivery.

"Hello, am I—" The tall man in the gray suit stopped and stared.

Truman adjusted his terrycloth turban. "Yes?"

The man cleared his throat and tried again. "Hello. Am I speaking with the, er, man of the house?"

202

"What is this about?"

"Uh—" The man revealed a clipboard, on which he focused his attention. "—we are going house-to-house to gauge how many men and women of the district are going to vote their conscience."

"Pardon?"

The man did not look up from his clipboard. "Do you intend to vote in the next election?"

"For whom?"

"I cannot tell you how to vote one way or the other. I just want to—"

"Wait—you're bothering me at home and you're not even here for a particular candidate?"

"No, sir." He kept staring at his clipboard clutched tightly in his hands. "The People Who Choose to Vote simply wants the men and women of this district to vote their conscience in the election."

"Huh."

"We're trying to find locals willing to welcome us into their homes, so that we can—"

"In what way?"

"Excuse me?"

"You said 'welcome us into their homes.'"

"Oh—we're looking for homes in the area to host our rallies. We want this to swell up as a legitimate grassroots movement before we start moving into the halls and arenas."

"Fine. Sign me up."

"Huh?" The man looked up. "What was that?"

Truman adjusted the towel on his head, and checked his robe. "You can have your meeting here. Go ahead and put this address down on your flyers and your website or whatever. When do you want to have your first home rally? How about tonight?"

The man gulped. "Tonight?"

"Why wait? This is a big house, there's ample parking along the street here. We got the room for as many people as you want."

"I suppose if we sent out an invitation through social media, we could get some folks here tonight."

"Sure you can!" Truman leaned out and flicked his eyes at the other houses. "When the neighbors see how popular your club is, they'll all want in, too."

The man's eyes grew big, and he grinned, too. "Right. Brilliant! Yes, Mr. —"

"Jim Polk."

The man pumped Truman's hand. "Yes, Mr. Polk! Thanks so much for your support."

"And you are?"

"Ralph. Ralph Hendricks."

"Nice to meet you, Ralph. How many do you think you can get to show up, Ralph?"

"Well, I suppose ten—"

"Oh, Ralph, you can do better than that."

"Well, if we make some calls, maybe fifteen—"

"If you want to make a good impression on the neighborhood, Ralph, you need at least twenty five people to show up. Do you think you can do that?"

Ralph smiled nervously and offered a tentative nod. "P-possibly."

"Just have everyone park along the street. But if they run out of room, they're free to pull around to the backyard."

"Great! Thank you, Mr. Polk."

A van pulled up at the end of the driveway. The driver got out and started unloading boxes onto a two-wheeled cart.

"My lunch is here. Do you like ravioli?"

The man furrowed his brow. "Actually, if we're going to get a group here tonight, I really need to get going."

"Of course. See you tonight!"

While his new friend Ralph was off making arrangements for a rally, Truman directed the deliveryman to wheel the cases of, well, everything, through the living room back to the kitchen. Handed the clipboard with the bill, Truman scribbled down a generous tip on the sheet and signed "James K. Polk" at the bottom.

The deliveryman glanced at the sheet. "Oh, we don't actually get tips this way."

"Oh, sorry." Truman made a show of checking the robe he had borrowed from Carlin, and was surprised to discover a roll of bills in the pocket. He peeled off a ten spot, and then another, and handed them to the man. "There you go."

The kitchen now had an island in the middle of the floor — a column of boxes, topped by an enormous orange circle. Ah, that would be the cheese.

Truman set aside the wheel of cheese and unstacked boxes until he found the case of ravioli and the box of magazines and one of the boxes that had beer in it. He got himself a can of ravioli, dug past all the women's magazines until he found a science magazine, and picked a beer that looked good and took a bottle. It was cold.

Microwaving the ravioli, he took his lunch and his magazine and his beer to the study. The library shelves were filled with baseball memorabilia. Truman set down the ravioli, magazine, and beer, adjusted his robe, and sat in the desk chair. When he got bored with the magazine, he started going through the drawers of the desk. He found what looked like some important papers in the file drawer. As he read them, trying unsuccessfully not to get sauce on them, he came across some interesting information regarding Jack Carlin's financial situation.

He was loaded. His father was Jefferson Ladron, president of LadronCo. And a prominent figure on the board for the *Nashville View*.

Truman set the paper down. One of his last columns for the paper was an expose on discrimination among management at LadronCo.

Jack Carlin Ladron's daddy had no doubt made a call to the owner of the *Nashville View*, demanding they get rid of that troublemaker Harry Truman. And while you're at it, how about they put his son in Truman's job?

His stomach gurgled again. He propped up his feet on the desk, sat back in the desk chair, and shut his eyes. He felt the turban slipping and he adjusted it.

He sat. He thought. He fumed.

After some period, Truman grabbed a phone book. He sat up and began flipping through the yellow pages. He found the listing for a particular business, pulled the cordless phone out of his robe pocket, and dialed the number. "Hello, Ace Swimming Pool? I need to place an order. How much extra to get started digging today?"

THIRTY-ONE

Following lunch, Truman decided to check out the back yard. While there was still, you know, a back yard.

Still wearing the robe and flopping turban, he went out the patio doors into the sun. He strode across the yard, his limp improving, his toes enjoying the warm grass, until he reached the shed.

The white building was corrugated metal, with black trim and roof. It was locked with a combination padlock. It took Truman a couple tries before he had it open.

"How are you this morning?" Calling from the next yard was an old woman dressed for gardening. She grinned with shiny dentures. On seeing Truman, her smile flickered. "You're not Mr. Carlin."

"No, ma'am. I'm his new, well, 'housemate.' If you know what I mean."

"You...live here?"

"Yes, ma'am."

The woman took on a stern tone. "You must know that we have a quiet community here. We don't go in for any wild shenanigans."

"No, ma'am, of course not. Jackie and I just want to be left to our privacy."

"We are very particular in this neighborhood."

"And I don't blame you. And I will be sure to mention that to all the kids at tonight's party."

She raised her eyebrows. "Party?"

"Don't you worry, we should be winding down sometime after midnight."

"The homeowners association does not allow any loud parties."

"Oh, come on, you're saying you and the husband don't have any shindigs now and again?"

"I assure you, Mr. McKenzie and myself only have friends over for tasteful get-togethers. Maybe cards and some wine. Never a 'wild party.'"

"Well, you can come on over tonight and have some fun on Jackie and me. With any luck, the pool will be installed by then."

"A pool!"

"Yes, they're supposed to get started today. I have no idea how long that takes—a day? A week? I've never had one before."

"The homeowners' association forbids the installation of any kind of swimming pools."

"Seriously?" Truman stood on his tiptoes and squinted around at the neighboring yards. "Not a one?"

"No, sir."

"Well, I guess Jackie and I will have to make a stand, won't we?"

"Mr.—"

"Harding. Call me Warren."

"Mr. Harding, I must tell you that I am very unhappy with what I am hearing."

"Is it your hearing aid? Do you need new batteries?"

"It is certainly not my hearing aid. It is the lout that Mr. Carlin has invited into his home. And I guarantee to you that I will report all this to the president of the homeowner's association. And with any luck, we will be calling you and Mr. Carlin in for a very strict discussion of what is acceptable in this neighborhood."

Truman put his hands in his robe pockets. He

rocked on the balls of his bare feet. "So, that's how it is, huh?"

"Yes, it is! And put some decent clothes on!" The woman stormed off for her house.

Truman turned back to the shed. It was dark inside, but he could make out a riding lawnmower, a shovel, a rake, some clippers, and then shelves and shelves of cans. Deciding some yard work might work off some of his energy, he chose the clippers; the lawnmower would become irrelevant after the diggers came.

He began clipping on one of the small trees along the border of the yard. He had no idea what he was doing, but was sure it would grow back. After all, they were trees.

He thought of the cordless phone in his robe pocket. Would it work this far out in the yard? He pulled it out and punched in a number from memory.

"*Nashville View.*"

"Hello, Tina. How's my sweet pea?"

"You have a lot of nerve calling me that."

"I thought you liked it."

"Truman? But the caller ID said—what are you doing at Carlin's?"

"I'm his houseguest. By the way, where is our friend Jack?"

"Not here. I don't know where he is."

"By any chance is he still out at the lake? Maybe chasing a certain story about a council person buying secret drugs?"

"Ah, that was you! I thought that lead sounded fishy. I told him the Waterdale lead made more sense, but he didn't think that Darla Lovell would really be out there."

"Somebody saw her?"

"Well, to be fair, we've gotten stacks of these messages. Cranks have claimed to have seen her all over — somebody even saw her with Elvis at the taco stand."

"With Bruce Lee and Jim Morrison, no doubt. Do you think Carlin fell into the lake or something?"

"I think he figured out it was a fake when I told him the city council had a meeting last night."

"Oh. I must have gotten my days mixed up. Of course, that still doesn't explain why he hasn't come home."

"By the way, watch out for bill collectors. They came in here looking for you. The boss told them to get lost, but then Carlin told them where you live."

"Bill collectors? What did they look like?"

"Well, one guy was like a football player or something. He was huge. And then the other guy was kind of small, and dressed like he was from the 1950s or something. Pin-striped suit and hat."

"Uh-huh."

"So watch for those guys."

"I'll be sure to do that. What's all that yelling in the background?"

"Oh, Mr. Withers is freaked out because he lost something."

"I see. Well, I guess I'll let you go."

"So, do you need me to run any more errands? It's the only real journalism I get to do."

"Not at the moment. I'll be in touch. Bye."

Truman switched off the phone. He looked at the tree, then the clippers on the grass. He switched on the phone and punched in some more numbers.

"Mike Wagner."

"Hey, I got to call off this week's poker game."

"Seriously? The wife will be off visiting her mother, so I was gonna be able to stay the whole game this time."

"Hmm, maybe we can relocate it. But my apartment is out."

"Well, we certainly can't meet at any of the other homes. You can imagine the problems that would cause for all of us."

"Yeah, I know."

"Because you know, me being a cop and them all being known members of organized crime."

"I get it. Maybe we can have it where I'm staying. A couple guys broke up my apartment."

"Seriously? Who did that?"

"One was a tall guy, built like a water buffalo with a cowboy hat and boots. Kept calling me 'Darling.' His handler was a small guy in a pinstriped suit and a hat. Do they sound familiar to you?"

"No. I don't know 'em. I guess you could flip through the books and see if you recognize anyone."

"Maybe."

"Do you need to come into headquarters here for police protection?"

"No, thanks. Besides, I'd hate to run into your FBI operation out there."

"Oh, they're not here. They've been spending all their time out at the record label."

"The record label?"

"Yeah, you know, because of that kidnapping case. It's a country singer that was grabbed. But the money was dropped off and she hasn't been returned yet. Bad news."

"I see."

"Say, I think I know why they were talking about you—do you remember a Special Agent Charles Murphy?"

"How could I forget? He shot my dog."

"It was your wife's dog—and he only injured it."

"I can still complain, can't I?"

"So you're certain you don't want police protection?"

"Well, when did you say that your wife is out of town?"

"She leaves Friday."

"Maybe I'll come stay with you this weekend."

"Wait, that's not what I—"

"See ya, Mike." Truman switched off the phone. In the next yard over, a couple kids ran out and started tossing around a ball. Truman waved. As soon as they saw the man in the robe and turban, they ran back inside.

Truman thought about something Wagner said. He thought about what he'd read in the paper about that kidnapping case. He thought about something the short guy said last night. He remembered the name of the record label from the newspaper.

He switched on the phone. He called information. He got the number he needed. He made the call.

"Unicorn Stinger Records."

"Hello, by any chance do you have an FBI agent named Murphy out there?"

"Just a second."

Silence.

"Hello, this is Murphy."

"Bow-Wow! How you been?"

"Who is this?"

"Why, this is Harry Truman. Don't tell me you forgot me?"

"Truman! Where are you?"

"Staying at a friend's. I just heard you were in town and thought it would be fun to catch up. Maybe talk over old times, you know? Shoot any more dogs lately?"

"No, I didn't—I—"

"Now, calm down. You'll have an aneurism."

"Fine. It's not too late to come clean, Truman. You can bring it all in now and we could make you a deal."

"I wondered."

"So that's why you called? You knew we'd offer you a deal?"

"Hmm? Oh, sorry, I meant something else. By the way, you should come by the apartment sometime. It's a mess, but—"

"Now, we had a warrant and everything."

"Uh-huh. By any chance, do you think I'm somehow involved in this kidnapping deal?"

"Don't try to play innocent, Truman."

"I would never do that. I'm just telling you I'm not involved. Or, to be more accurate, I am just a bystander."

"You'll never get a deal talking like that."

"I'm not looking for a deal, I just want people to stop barging into my home and destroying my apartment. It's a sad world when a man is afraid to sleep in his own bed."

"We did what we had to do."

"So, you're telling me that you sent those two

men?"

"What two men? What are you talking about?"

"What are *you* talking about?"

"Look, when we brought out the team to search your apartment, we had a warrant. And why am I explaining myself to you? Anything we broke in the proper course of our search was simply an unfortunate happenstance in the pursuit of justice."

"Well, I simply must go. But I am sure you had enough time to run your trace. Goodbye, Bow-Wow."

Truman switched off he phone and inserted it into the pocket of the robe. He was thinking when a voice bellowed from the side of the house.

"Hey! You the guy who ordered a swimming pool?"

THIRTY-TWO

FBI Special Agent Murphy and FBI Special Agent Reed were in the car, racing across town to Jack Carlin's house. All told, it was about two hours since they had gotten the call from Harry Truman—they had travelled from Music Row to the courthouse downtown, stopped in for a quick talk with the judge to get the warrant signed, then on to the house in historic Franklin.

"What a break," Murphy said. "I can't believe that squab would make a tactical error like that."

"Yeah," Reed grumbled. "Seems too good to be true."

"Fortune favors the prepared. We were ready for the call, and we traced it."

"We had caller ID."

"That's a kind of tracing."

"And he told you that he knew you'd be tracing the call."

"Well, sure. The arrogance of the criminal mind."

"Or somebody messing with you."

Murphy squinted at the other agent. "You really don't get it, do you? If you would just pay a little closer attention to how it's done, you might go places."

Reed matched him, squint for squint. "And I suppose you're the one who's going to show me how it's done? You're out chasing this Truman character, instead of pursuing a legitimate line of—"

"What does it take for you to see that Truman is guilty as sin? He's clearly involved in the kidnapping of that sweet little girl. Besides, he ran—an innocent man doesn't run."

"He might if he's got an 800-pound gorilla bashing in his front door. That might make an innocent man run away."

"Not if it's the 800-pound gorilla of justice—okay, I'm going to drop the analogy there. But it's justice that bashed in the front door of Harry Truman, and if he were innocent, he would have been there waiting."

"Not all innocent people were home last night."

"Of course they were."

"Were you at home last night?"

"No, but I was at the—" Murphy glared. "Shut up."

Reed smiled.

"And if there were any doubts before, surely that call from Truman would have made you see what was what. Clearly a guilty man calling to unload his conscience."

"I thought you said it was arrogance."

"That, too. All of that. Guilt. Arrogance. And a slip of the tongue."

"He made a special call to have a slip of the tongue?"

"Well, sure. Of course. And now we know that this Jack Carlin person is his partner. You heard Truman say he was hiding out with his accomplice."

"Actually, he said he was staying at a friend's. Which, given what happened to his apartment, no jury in the world would blame him. He had to go somewhere."

"Criminals only make friends with accomplices." Murphy grunted. "I cannot believe we had that Carlin in our hands and we let him go. I should have grabbed him. I knew that innocent act of his was a put-on."

"We don't know that."

"We know enough to have a warrant."

"I still don't understand why that judge keeps listening to you. Does he have a thing against Truman, too?"

Murphy's eyes flickered to the other man and away. "That's beside the point."

"And now that we have this warrant, are we going to trash this man's home like we trashed Truman's?"

"We do what it takes to pursue justice."

"Meanwhile, that poor girl could still be out there somewhere. The clock is ticking, and we're too busy rocketing off after this Truman to do any real investigating. We need to go back and figure out where she might be. And, I'm telling you, that Buddy Powell looks awfully fishy to me."

"Well, I'm the senior agent here, and I'm saying that we go after Truman. And I'm going to pursue this kidnapping case to the logical end. If that means busting up the home of this Jack Carlin, well, he shouldn't have gotten involved in kidnapping and probably murder."

Reed bit his lip. He was all answered out.

The entourage reached historic Franklin, home to all sorts of Civil War memorials. Within a few minutes, they had reached the residential area and found the neighborhood they were looking for. The block. The street.

At the address, the car pulled up along the curb and the men got out. The van pulled up behind the car and a series of agents in full combat gear tumbled out. Murphy went to the trunk of the car and spread out some sheets like it was a desk. The large group gathered behind him and waited silently for orders. "Okay, folks, we don't want that jerk to escape us again."

"Or simply not be home."

"Shut up, Reed. Now there are lights on in that window, so we can assume the subject is home. Okay, I want you three to flank left. Then you three go around the right side of the house. The rest circle around and come in from the back. Let me know when you're in position. Now, go!"

As the combat agents shot off to follow their orders, Reed nodded to the sheets spread out on the trunk. "So, what are these?"

"They're what you call 'props.' It helps me clear my head."

"So they don't hold any significance whatsoever?"

"Should they?"

Reed shrugged. "I guess not."

"Look, the light switched off and turned on in another room. So at least somebody's home this time."

"Or he set up some timers to automatically switch on and off the lights."

"Why are you always so down on everything?"

"Anytime I see the FBI running around like a bunch of morons, it makes me uncomfortable."

"You got a smart mouth."

"At least I can take some comfort that we're not all like that."

The agents around back reported a large hole in the backyard. Murphy sneered, "What more evidence do you need? He's digging a bunker!"

"I can't imagine that's right."

Murphy grabbed the bullhorn and felt the heft of it in his grip. He grinned like a six-year-old and put the device to his lips and spoke. It exploded with feedback. He made an adjustment and tried again. "Attention, Harry Truman! This is the Federal Bureau of Investigation. We know you're in there, Truman—and we've got the place surrounded! You've got thirty seconds to come outside here with your hands over your head!" He pulled down the bullhorn and grinned to the other agent. "That should put the fear of God in him."

"If he's even there."

The two men stood and waited for anyone to come out. Or peek out the curtains. Or respond or even react in any way. Ten seconds passed. Nothing.

Reed glanced around at the nearby houses. "Well, you got the attention of the neighbors."

"If they're law-abiding citizens, then they don't mind."

"And if they do mind?"

"We can always start a file on them." Murphy put the bullhorn to his lips. "You've got ten more seconds, Truman!"

A small crowd was forming behind the two agents. Reed nodded. "Good evening!"

A woman called out, "What'd Mr. Carlin do? Is he running a Meth lab?"

Murphy snarled, "Aiding and harboring a Federal criminal, an accomplice in a Federal crime—"

"Well," Reed jumped in, "we're still investigating that."

"Shut up." Murphy turned to the crowd and

barked, "Get out of here! These are dangerous fugitives! They could start shooting at any second!"

Reed motioned toward Carlin's house. "There's nobody there."

"Oh, they're there. They're hiding like the cowards they are. We just got here before they finished building their bunker."

"I bet they're just digging a swimming pool."

An elderly man stepped up. "What was that? Did you say swimming pool?"

"Probably."

"The homeowner's association has a strict policy against that sort of thing! Mr. Carlin will certainly have to explain himself."

Reed scratched his head. "His house is surrounded by the FBI and you're more worried about a hole in the backyard?"

"It is a strict policy."

Murphy stared at the house, his shoulders slumped. "Why don't they come out? Even if Truman isn't there, everybody else should all still come out."

Reed said, "Maybe you should specify that. After all, you said 'Truman.'"

Murphy nodded. He cleared his throat and yelled into the bullhorn again. "Attention anyone in the house! Whether or not you are Harry Truman, you are commanded to come out of that house with your hands up! This is your last warning!" He started to put down the horn and brought it back for, "This is the F-B-I." He clearly annunciated "F-B-I" to avoid any misunderstanding.

Ten seconds passed. Nothing.

Murphy looked at Reed, who shrugged. Murphy

pulled the mic to his lips and gave the other agents the "go" order.

At the front door, two agents used a battering ram to smash their way inside, and led the way into the foyer. They were confronted with two sets of stairs — one leading up and one down.

Murphy, his gun at the ready, silently motioned for one of the padded agents to lead upward. He pointed for Reed and the other padded agent to go downstairs.

Reed nodded without rolling his eyes, and led the padded agent down the stairs. He hadn't even drawn his weapon. In the furnished basement, the couch and love seat and chairs created a semi-circle in front of a large television. Along the back wall was a wet bar. The walls were wood-paneled — no, they were covered with plastic faux wood paneling.

The padded agent looked around and pulled up the visor on his helmet. "What now?"

Reed let out a heavy sigh. "I guess we're supposed to look for hiding places."

"Down here?"

"Mm-hmm." Reed headed back for the stairs and saw a door. It opened to an unfinished part of the basement, jammed full of boxes. And a bicycle. "Anyone hiding back here? Didn't think so." He pulled the door shut and went for the stairs. "We're done down here."

Upstairs, someone had gone through and flipped on all the lights in the house. The agents who'd entered from behind the house had left the kitchen door in splinters. They'd also tracked in fresh earth from the excavation out back.

Reed shook his head, but he held his tongue.

There was no point. This was Murphy's operation. It would be his name on the complaint.

There was a racket down the hall, and Reed followed the noise until he reached the den. The white couch was covered with stains, and the coffee table overflowed with crusty dishes and partially eaten food. The patio doors had also been smashed in, glass and wood now strewn across the carpet.

Murphy was instructing the others to beat on the walls looking for secret rooms. They'd punched several holes in the fragile plaster.

Reed stormed up to Murphy. "You've got to be kidding me! Do you really consider this necessary?"

Murphy snorted. "Anything for justice."

"This isn't justice. This is just damage."

"Collateral damage."

"No. Just damage." Reed was struggling to find the words to convince the other agent to stop the madness.

There was a loud clang. Everyone stopped and looked around.

Reed frowned. "What is that? Did you guys set off some kind of alarm?"

Murphy shook his head. "That's not like any alarm I ever heard."

It sounded again, and Reed realized it was possibly the doorbell. He and Murphy both trudged through the debris and made their way to the front door. Reed opened it to find a man in a suit standing there.

The man looked from Murphy to Reed and smiled uncertainly. "Hello, is Mr. Polk here?"

Murphy and Reed exchanged a glance. "Who?"

"Jim Polk. He invited us to have our meeting

here tonight."

Murphy growled, "No, you can't have your—" He stopped when he noticed all the cars parking outside—in the driveway, along the street, pulling up into the yard. "Who are all these people?"

THIRTY-THREE

When the FBI raced out of the offices of Unicorn Stinger Records, Truman was driving in exactly the opposite direction. His guess had been that Special Agent Charles "Bow-Wow" Murphy simply would not stand for getting his nose tweaked like that. So, as soon as he got off the phone with Bow-Wow, Truman had dressed, got in his car, and drove out to Music Row.

Parked along the curb across the street, he spent a few minutes watching the label office. It was an old house that had been converted into a business.

When he decided it looked reasonably safe, he got out of the car and popped the trunk. He grabbed a set of coveralls, pulled them over his street clothes, and zipped up. He dug for the mustache, but it was a little mangled, so he left it. He grabbed a big empty water cooler jug and slung it over his shoulder. It hid his face from one side, and gave him an excuse to skulk around an office.

He slammed the trunk closed, and carried the big empty jug across the street, continuing to favor his injured leg. He tried the front door. It was locked. He rapped his knuckles on the pane, and glanced around to see whether anyone was passing on the sidewalk or the street. Nobody answered.

He squinted through the little window in the door, then leaned and squinted through the picture window. There was nobody in the front room.

It was odd that Bow-Wow hadn't left at least one agent behind to man the phones. In case, you know, the real kidnapper called.

Glancing around again for any passerby, he

stepped down to the grass and went around the side of the building. Still carrying the jug, he got to the back door and knocked again. Nobody answered.

Hidden by the unruly row of bushes lining the empty parking lot, he set down the jug and got to work on the door. He was inside in a matter of seconds. He checked for an alarm, but it hadn't been set.

Standing in the kitchen, he held his breath and listened. All he heard was the sound of an empty house. He grabbed a chair and sat at the table. The centerpiece was a small wicker basket filled with assorted packets — salt, sugar, sugar substitute, tea. Truman dropped the samples packets, wondering what he was expecting to find. Why was he even here?

He went and opened the refrigerator. It was jammed with cans of store brand soda pop. There was one of those clear plastic clamshell containers with somebody's leftover lunch. Ooh — taco salad — but he was still full of ravioli, so he set it back and closed the door.

In the living room, he closed the blinds and flicked on the lamp. He went to the receptionist desk and started digging through the drawers. Appointment book. Address book. Paperwork. Nothing really jumped out at him.

He flipped through the appointment book. One of the label's artists was scheduled to be in the studio next week. Hardly earth-shattering news.

He flipped through the address book. A lot of media contacts. Music industry personnel. The dentist.

Moving his snooping to the big office in the

back, he found a series of plaques on the wall, all inscribed to a man named Buddy Powell. Some of the plaques were Gold or Platinum records awarded for album sales, some marked hit radio singles, and others just honored Mr. Powell's status in the music industry.

None of the plaques had been awarded more recently than about ten years ago. Squinting at the names of all the recording artists, he noted that many of them had already fallen out of public favor. Those still working in music had moved on to bigger record labels.

Truman sat in the big chair. He kicked off and spun the chair a few times. Whee.

Stopping just short of dizziness, he set to checking the desk. Some mechanical contraption was hooked up to the phone, no doubt so the FBI could monitor all incoming calls.

Digging through the scribbled notes on Buddy's desk, Truman found a flyer which listed the address for the Unicorn Stinger recording studio, all the way out in Waterdale. *Waterdale.* Where had he just heard that word? Right, Tina had mentioned something about a crank call.

A little further into his excavation, he found a note indicating the amount of the ransom demanded by the kidnapper or kidnappers. It made him stop: Whoever had monkeyed around with his bank account had been working with the exact same dollar figure.

He sat back in the chair and thought on that. What in the world could it mean? And how in the world do you climb out of a hole when you can't even figure out who had dug it—or how?

A set of notes were labeled "Darla Lovell Homecoming Tour." From what Truman had seen and heard of the artist, she was just a kid starting out—under normal circumstances too young for any kind of "homecoming" tour. This must be for when she got home from the kidnappers.

Wagner said the ransom was paid, but the girl was not returned. That was never a good sign—in his career as a crime reporter, Truman had written too many grim reminders that a kidnap victim's return was a rarity. And the longer the time before the victim was returned, the lower the odds they ever came back.

So Buddy's plans for this "homecoming tour" meant that he had high hopes for a miracle. It broke Truman's heart.

Skimming the printout, Truman saw that dates had already been booked. Venues locked up. Tickets being sold. That was a lot of faith.

Here was another spreadsheet, this one indicating airplay for Darla Lovell's radio single. Apparently, the tragedy was doing wonders for her on the airwaves.

Truman felt a twinge of mixed feelings. It seemed tacky to capitalize on the young singer's misfortune like this. On the other hand, maybe this was how a man like Buddy Powell worked through his grief

Still, it all made Truman feel a little icky. He set down the spreadsheets and pushed them aside. He saw a yellow ribbon with some typescript along the edge. He didn't bother to read it.

In this drawer were some odds and ends. A stapler. Boxes of paper clips. Ink pens. A disposable cell phone. Post-it notes. And then some —

Wait.

Truman picked up the disposable cell phone and looked at it. Why would a man like Buddy Powell want a disposable cell phone? The few answers that came to mind were dependant on whether the man was married, and/or had some business or addiction he wanted to keep a secret.

But even those did not explain why Buddy Powell would keep the phone in this drawer in this office. He looked at the office telephone — and all the wires attached to it by the FBI. For recording.

Truman didn't get any further than that when he heard a rattle at the front door. He glanced at his watch — was Bow-Wow and company back already?

Truman jumped from the chair and ran across the office to switch off the light. Then he realized he didn't know his way around in the dark. He cursed, switched on the light, and ran for the hall.

The front door popped open. A voice called out, "Who's here?"

In the kitchen, Truman slid on the linoleum floor and slammed into the table. He stumbled and fell on his bad ankle.

The voice called out again. "Whoever that is, hold it right there!"

Truman crawled to his feet and got to the back kitchen door. Sweating hands fumbled with the knob, and he finally got the door open.

A man in uniform appeared in the kitchen. "Hey!"

Truman tripped on the porch, tumbled down the stairs, and sprawled out in the back parking lot. The concrete hurt.

The uniformed man stood at the door, shining a flashlight down at him. "Stop right there!"

Truman took a deep breath, braced himself against the pain in his ankle, and crawled to his feet. He hobbled for the edge of the pavement. If the uniformed man was fast—or, for that matter, was moving at all—he had a problem.

At the car, Truman heard the man gaining, huffing and puffing. Truman, huffing and puffing himself, got in the car. Turned the key in the ignition. Sped off.

In the rearview mirror, the man in uniform pointed his flashlight. Would he get in his car and follow? Would he call for backup?

Truman didn't wait and find out. He stepped on the gas and sped down the one-way street. He turned left onto a connecting street, and got on the other parallel one-way street.

He got to the roundabout—the one with the big, naked statues. He drove around it once. Twice. Three times.

Blinking himself into clarity, Truman regained his bearings and sped off down one of the side roads. There were no flashing lights behind him, so he slowed to the speed limit—no sense calling attention to himself.

He pulled into the parking lot behind a Jamaican restaurant. Stumbling inside, he grabbed a table as far back as possible. He ordered the first of what he assumed would be several drinks. As he tried to calm his nerves, he noted that he still had Buddy Powell's disposable cell phone in his pocket.

Around the third drink, it finally hit him that he had no place to sleep that night.

THIRTY-FOUR

When Jack Carlin's life had flashed before his eyes, he was not a happy man. Granted, some of that unhappiness may have stemmed from the circumstances—you know, being certain he was going to die and all—but the flickers of memory that paraded before him during the event had left him nonplussed as well.

So now, as he drifted in nothingness, regrets continued to poke at him. Was this all there was to the afterlife? Floating? Being poked by the sharp edges of dissatisfied memories? No St. Peter, no pearly gates, no Marilyn Monroe to welcome him? If this was what happened when you died, then all the philosophers and ministers of the world should have done a better job preparing him. Not to mention all those Loony Tunes.

During the fatal event, the overarching theme of his flashbacks had been that Jack Carlin had deserved better. From his father. From his third grade teacher. From the groundskeeper at his boyhood home. From Mr. Withers at the paper. From his co-workers. Not to mention from God and the world and everyone else.

Yes, Jack Carlin determined, in life he'd deserved way more respect. If he were somehow given another chance back on Earth, he would make a point to tell everyone exactly that.

He'd march into Withers' office. "You should respect me," he'd say. Maybe he'd pound the desk. "I'm going to be running this place someday, so you'd better stop belittling me!" Oh, yeah, and "Stop letting that idiot Truman keep correcting me!"

And then there were his co-workers — in particular, that little watermelon Tina Davis. She barely gave him the time of day. If he were granted a chance to go back, he would go right up and say, "You better treat me right." He probably wouldn't pound her desk, because the angle in that small cubicle was kind of awkward. "One day, I'll own all this, and then you'll be sorry."

Well, okay, he would need to come up with something better than "You'll be sorry." That line probably wouldn't get the chicks to come back to the ol' bachelor pad. He needed something more along the lines of "Your loss if you lose out." Or "How about we get better acquainted over the lunch hour, if you know what I mean?" And give her that wink he'd practiced in the mirror.

Of course, if the afterlife here turned out to be eternal, then he'd have all kinds of time to work out the speech. It's not like he had anything else to do here.

And then there was Harry Truman. The devil himself. "You did this to me, Truman," Jack would say. "You killed me."

Well, maybe he wouldn't say that. Not if he were actually alive to say it. But as long as Truman was in the way, the world would never give Jack Carlin the respect that Jack Carlin deserved.

A funnel of light opened before him. He floated in its direction. He wanted desperately to paddle toward it, but found his limbs were numb. Did he even have a body anymore?

He floated closer. Closer.

Eventually, he was in a bright, white room. There was the sound of beeping. And breathing. He wiggled his nose. Heaven smelled like…ammonia.

He was in a hospital room. So he wasn't dead. Huh.

But not being a resident of the hereafter produced its own set of questions. Carlin's thinking was still foggy, but fractured memories began to fit together into larger pictures. The ox man had attacked him and Carlin had run. He jumped out the window and discovered, then, that he was on the third floor. And then he was falling toward the parking lot.

And then he was here in the hospital. It was hard to think. Everything was hazy. Hoping to get a sense of the room, he struggled to turn his head. He tried to get up. He tried to move his arms and legs. He tried to call for help.

He couldn't do any of that.

Carlin needed to somehow take stock of his situation. With a heroic effort, he blinked heartily, trying to force himself to think more clearly. To sharpen his awareness to crystal clarity. With some amount of pain in his eyeballs, he looked downward, as downward as he could, and saw straps and casts and wrappings. He counted the casts.

One. Two. Three. Four.

Both arms. Both legs. In casts.

He was in traction.

He tried to yell. He couldn't open his mouth. Why was that? Had he been drugged? Was he maybe still too numb to move his muscles? What had they done to him?

He blinked, if only to prove to himself he could move something. It hurt, but the pain shoved a helpful spike into his brain, shocking him awake.

As the pain grew, one hated name blazed into his brain. Truman! This was all Truman's fault. Somehow, somewhere, Truman had done this to him. And if Jack Carlin was alive, that meant he could get even. And if he could get even, then he would get even if it was the last thing he would ever do.

He turned his attention again to the present situation. So, for whatever reason, Jack Carlin was completely immobilized. All he could do was look. So he looked.

With a great amount of concentration, he twisted his eyes in the general direction of left. There was a window over there, sun streaming through the slits in the blinds. Under the window was one of those heating/cooling units like Carlin had seen in cheap motels in the movies. As a privileged child, he had never been exposed to such rustic machinery in person.

With another burst of concentration, he twisted his eyes in the general direction of right. He saw another hospital bed. There was a man in it. The man was wearing a hospital gown and he was sleeping.

Hanging from the ceiling was a small TV. It was turned to a courtroom show. Carlin wished with all his might that he could change the channel. But, alas, he had not returned from the great beyond with the ability to do that.

Now, with a great deal of concentration, Jack Carlin scanned the whole room, moving his eyes to and fro. With a growing sense of sour frustration, he became sure of the horrible truth.

There was nobody here. Not his family, not his friends, not well wishers. Nobody. Just this loser in the next bed snoring.

Why was there nobody else here? Didn't they know he was Jack Carlin? He was an important man! He was going to inherit a media empire one day!

The second problem was that there were no flowers. No bouquets, no balloons, no boxes of candy, no stuffed animals, no cards. Nothing. What was wrong with people? Under normal circumstances, Jack Carlin deserved to be showered with gifts — how much more so when he was here at death's door?

The third problem: He was not even in a private room. Like he was a common man off the street. What was he, blue collar?

And then the worst problem of all: Why were no medical personnel standing by? Didn't the hospital know a VIP was in here? That Jack Carlin could buy and sell any of them any day of the week — and, once he got out of here, would likely do so?

He was really wishing a nurse were here. She could scratch that itch festering inside his cast. And then she could wipe the sweat off his lip. And then she could give him a sponge bath.

He tried to look for the call box. The buzzer thing. The remote. What was that called? He needed to demand a nurse. This itch was getting progressively worse.

With effort, he finally saw the box dangling overhead, hanging by a cord. Immobilized like he was, the device might as well have been thrown into the Grand Canyon. He could not possibly reach it.

Maybe he could just call for a nurse the old fashioned way. He tried again to yell. To speak. To mumble. No good.

With a great deal of focus, he could turn his head a little. A bit. A smidgen. He looked with his eyes as hard as he could look to the right. There was a phone on the nightstand next to his bed.

If only he could call for someone. Anyone.

Maybe he could call the offices at the paper. In this condition, maybe he would finally get some sympathy from his editor.

Maybe Tina would finally give him the time of day like she meant it.

Yes, maybe he could turn this experience to his advantage. He mulled over the possibilities with Tina and was warmed by his impure imagination.

His thoughts were broken by the entrance of two people. His heart fell when he noticed they were men—and not even doctors. They were strangers, a man in a frayed brown suit and a man in a sharp, dark suit.

Carlin was a little surprised to see them come to the foot of his bed and look at him. One of them seemed familiar.

"So he's in traction here," the man in the frayed brown suit was saying. "Fractures in his arms and legs. Jaw wired shut. Three broken ribs."

"Uh-huh," the man in the sharp dark suit replied. "But what does that have to do with us?"

"Well, John Doe here isn't in any condition to tell us who he is. He didn't have any ID when they brought him in, and his prints don't show up in any of our databases."

"And—?"

"He was found right outside an apartment building where you fellas had just had one of your, um, incursions. Right?"

236

"One of our—"

"Witnesses claim they saw you boys bust down the door of one of the apartments. Then right after that, they found this guy all broken and bleeding on the parking lot outside. It's like he was thrown out of a third story window. You guys were on the third story, right?"

Carlin was only vaguely following the discussion. He was attempting to blink a message at them. How did you blink "S-O-S"? Or "H-E-L-P"?

The man in the dark suit turned toward Carlin and regarded him. Suddenly, Carlin remembered where he saw him before.

Special Agent Reed squinted right into the patient's eyes. His jaw dropped. "I think I know who this is."

THIRTY-FIVE

Truman self-consciously touched the fake beard, and pulled the ratty overcoat close around himself. He was at the Fifth Avenue Shelter, where he planned to hide while he sorted out some things. He was either a genius or he had simply sunk as low as he ever could.

The entrance procedure was more rigorous than he'd expected: He had been checked for weapons, checked for drug use, checked whether he was currently drunk or high, checked whether he suffered from any kind of violent mental illness.

The process wasn't really all that intrusive, but enough to make a man nervous when he wants to remain anonymous. He must not have been exceptional in this regard, because without any prompting, the helpers—what do you call them, missionaries?—assured him that his anonymity would be protected.

There was one little kerfuffle when he bumped into Geneva Phillips. She'd looked past the fake beard right away, her eyes widening. She threatened to have him thrown out, but he pulled her aside.

"Think of it this way," he said, "if you help me, your father would hate it."

She sighed. "Fine. So, what'd you find out?"

"About—?"

"Whoever you made out that check to."

"Oh! I haven't had a chance yet to look it up."

She frowned. "So, what's taking you?"

"It's not exactly like I've been sitting around. I had visitors. And then this other thing happened."

"Like what?"

He shook his head. "I don't think you want to become an accessory after the fact."

She frowned again. "I see. Well, will you please try not to cause any trouble here?"

"I'll be good. Scout's honor."

"That's the Vulcan thing."

"So they tell me."

She made a face and walked away, leaving him free to mingle among the homeless at the shelter. Which, he was pained to realize, included him, too — he was, for all intents and purposes, also homeless.

And then he ran into Dawkins again. The weasel acknowledged Truman with a frown. "A beard now? Man, who are you supposed to be this time?"

"Be cool, man," Truman said in the grooviest tone of voice he could muster. "I'm just here for a little while and then I'll be gone."

Dawkins nibbled on one of his fingernails. "So you aren't, um, here to see me or anything?"

"No, I'm just here because—" Truman shrugged. "Because. That's all. Honest."

"Uh-huh."

"Look, if you don't believe me, how about I go this way and you go that way, and we don't talk again until the morning."

"What happens then?"

"If we're feeling civil, we say 'Good morning.' But if you don't feel up to it, you're not required or anything."

"Actually, we are."

"Huh?"

"It's one of the rules of the shelter—'Say good morning to God, say good morning to each other.'"

"You can't be serious."

"See if I ain't."

With that, they parted ways. Truman wandered off toward the gym, where some of the shelter's guests were playing a game of half-court basketball.

***

When it was time for bed, Truman found an unoccupied bunk and piled in, his ratty overcoat pulled up tight around him for protection. At lights out, he shut his eyes and listened to the building. The aging central air made a racket. At occasional intervals, water rushed through pipes in the walls.

Truman controlled his breathing, not so much to sleep as to think. He needed to sort through all the things that had led him here to this place.

A large sum of money was misplaced, accidentally or purposefully, by person or persons unknown. The dollar amount of this money was the same as the dollar amount demanded in ransom by the kidnappers of country singer Darla Lovell.

This money—whether or not it was the actual ransom—had temporarily been placed in the bank account of one Harry Truman, an unemployed journalist. The money had been deposited into his checking account without the account holder's knowledge or consent.

A few days later, the money was somehow removed from the account. Again without his knowledge or consent.

Whether or not this money was the "lost" ransom money—and the dollar amount was too much of a coincidence to ignore the possibility— several people seemed to be operating under the assumption that it was. A couple of thugs. The FBI.

There had to be an answer. It was just a matter of fitting all the pieces into place, and then he'd be able to see the picture.

Truman remembered the little man from the IRS. Marion Russell. The man, who turned out to be from all the way out at the Memphis branch, had taken off from his office without telling his co-workers where he was going. (Whatever happened to him, anyway?) Although the man was certainly annoying, and perhaps knew more than he was saying, it did not seem likely that he would have caused any of this.

Truman thought about his conversations with Mike Wagner at the police. He'd known Wagner a while, and they'd been friends for a lot of that time. Wagner had been an invaluable help with the column at the paper — a fact that Wagner never wanted his superiors to discover. If Wagner had heard anything on the street, he'd more than likely have passed along the information. Mike was always good about that.

Truman thought of his first visit to the Fifth Avenue Shelter. Thought of the African American goddess named Geneva Phillips. Her father had turned out to be a very powerful man, one with a very powerful dislike of Truman. But any way you sliced it, Truman just could not imagine that her father would have done something like this. He was the sort of man who, when he chose to squash a bug, just paid a man to whack it with a shoe and be done with it. He didn't seem the type to go such a circuitous route.

Truman thought of Dawkins. Strange running into him here at the shelter, wasn't it? Truman thought of how they bumped into one another before, when Dawkins had blown Truman's cover.

Truman thought of his visit to his contact at the bank. His visit to his contact with the mob. Neither conversation had proven fruitful.

Truman thought of those crazy thugs who had broken up his apartment. That big ox man throwing Truman around like a rag doll, calling him "Darling." What in the world were they really asking? If only Truman could have had a chance to interview them, maybe he could have gotten a better handle on why they thought he had the money.

Truman thought of Jack Carlin. Truman thought of FBI Special Agent Charlie "Bow-Wow" Murphy. Their roles in this whole ordeal were as yet undefined. Carlin told those goons how to find Truman's home. Carlin was also still missing as of the last time Truman was at his home.

Meanwhile, the FBI had left behind all kinds of paper trails at their local headquarters. And Bow-Wow did not seem to have sharpened any during his long period of banishment.

Truman sat up suddenly, banging his head on the bunk above him. Ouch.

Head spinning, he rolled over and crawled out the bunk onto the floor. He righted himself and stood, stumbling out to the hall. He went from room to room whispering one name loudly: "Dawkins!"

In the fourth room, he found the man and shook him awake. Dawkins squinted at him. "Wh-what is it, man?"

Truman said, "Tell me that part again about the check."

THIRTY-SIX

Dawkins acted too groggy to understand what Truman was asking. So Truman dragged him down from his bunk, out to the hall, and down to the gymnasium for a private chat.

Inside the big, dark room, Truman fumbled for the switch on the wall and then there was light. He looked over at Dawkins slumped against the wall. Truman growled, "Okay, spill it."

Dawkins, who apparently drooled in his sleep, wiped his jaw with his sleeve. "Why'd you drag me out of bed, man?"

"It's time for you to come clean."

"I didn't do nothin', man."

Truman chewed his lip a second, thinking of another approach. "How come you never cashed my check?"

"Huh?" Dawkins' eyes flickered with recognition. "I don't know what you're talking about."

Truman gave an exaggerated sigh. "A few months ago, I came to you for some information. I was checking out some details for the column—"

"But you don't even do that column no more."

"I was checking up on Jack Carlin's column—making corrections—and I needed some information. I came to you, because, low-life that you are, you do a lot of scurrying around. Sometimes you manage to overhear a lot of the right people."

"Hey, that sounded like an insult."

Truman held up a hand. "And you provide a valuable service. Most of the time. But this last time I came to you, I no longer had the company card."

"You didn't say a word until after I came through. Didn't even pay me."

"Of course I paid you! But I no longer had the expense account, so I had to write a personal check — to you."

"Okay, fine. Is that any reason to drag me out of bed? I thought maybe you had something important to talk about."

"But the funny thing is, Dawkins, you never cashed the check."

The other man looked at his fingernails. "Yeah?"

"The first couple statements I had some trouble reconciling my balance and noticed it. And then somewhere along the way I stopped thinking about it." Truman's eyes narrowed and bore into the other man. "But now I am thinking about it. And I need to know — why didn't you cash the check, Dawkins? Huh?"

The man glanced away. "Maybe I didn't want to take your money, you being out of work and all. Maybe I just wanted to do you a favor."

"You wouldn't do a favor for your grandma."

"You don't know my grandma."

"Why didn't you cash the check, Dawkins?"

The other man scratched the peach fuzz on his chin. "Look, man, I don't got no bank account. Right? So I got nowhere to deposit it. Nobody would cash your check for me, see?"

"Surely you could have taken it somewhere."

"Well, I couldn't."

"Uh-huh."

"Honest! Look, Truman, it's late. Can I get back to bed now? Maybe we can talk about this tomorrow?"

"You used the account information on my check to make a deposit into my bank account. Didn't you?"

"Are you nuts? Why would I do that?"

"But the point on which I am still a little unclear is how you then were able to transfer $500,000 to the mission."

"Shut up, man!" Dawkins moved closer to Truman and spoke in a low, conspiratorial voice. "People around this place hear things. I don't want nobody to get the wrong idea."

"Fine. Then tell me, Dawkins, where'd you get the money?"

The man sighed. "I just had a couple business deals come in. That's all."

"You don't run in circles where you get hold of that much cash." Truman tilted his head. "Did you grab it off the mob? Maybe snatch it from a bagman or something?"

His eyes grew wide. "You think I'm crazy? I'd never do something like that."

"Then why are you in hiding?"

"Well, okay, but I'd never steal that much from the mob at one time!"

"Fine, then, you didn't steal it from the mob. Did someone give you the money to launder? Maybe you thought you could filter it through my account to try and clean it out a little?"

"What? No, man, it wasn't like that."

"Then what was it like? Just tell me."

The man sighed. "Fine. A couple guys came around and asked me to hide some cash for them."

"Hmm, I don't think I believe that."

"What do you want?"

"Look, Dawkins, I have had the worst couple of days in my life. I'm not above turning you over to save my own skin—if it comes down to a choice between you and me, I'll pick me every time. So tell me what's going on, before I drag you down to hand you over to the FBI. Or Fat Tony."

"Wait—what? No, man, no reason to get him involved!"

"Then spill it. Right here, right now."

Dawkins, his back to the wall, slid to the floor like his knees had given out on him. He sat on the hard wooden gymnasium floor, staring at his bare feet. "Fine."

Truman crouched and sat on his heels. "Go ahead."

"So a couple guys came in here a few weeks ago—maybe last month—and they had some kind of score. They were sort of hanging around the shelter here, kind of feeling out which of these homeless guys might be good for cheap labor."

"Who were they?"

"I don't know, man, I never spoke to them directly. But then the word got around that they were some kind of music industry types."

"Fine. Go on."

"Guys worked at a record label or something. And so they visited here at the shelter a few times, and somehow decided they could trust Hector and Ray. So they had this whole plan worked out—it was supposed to be a secret, but Hector and Ray were both kinda loose with their mouths, if you know what I mean."

"Uh-huh."

"They were supposed to be the front men for

some kinda publicity stunt. And then something about a suitcase at a drop point, and Hector and Ray were supposed to pick up the case and bring it back here and give it to the other two guys. The ones from the record label."

"What was it all about?"

"I told you, some publicity stunt. So they gave Hector and Ray a few bucks to get a cab or a car or something for the thing. But here's where the music biz guys made their mistake: There are some guys who can't handle getting a few bucks."

"I see."

"So the night of the thing, the guys had bought a few bottles of wine, and were pretty sloshed. So I offered to drive for them."

"What happened?"

Dawkins shrugged. "I drove for them. It was hard following the directions, but we got to the place and it turned out to be like a picnic table in a little park, way off the road. Seemed like a weird place to do a publicity stunt."

"Uh-huh."

"Well, there was a suitcase there on the table. Just sitting out there, on the table, in the middle of nowhere. I get it and take it back to the car. By this point, the guys are completely sleeping in the back of the car. So I decided to take a look inside the suitcase and see what a publicity stunt looks like."

Truman was getting a sick feeling. "What happened?"

"The suitcase was stuffed full of bills, man. More bills than I ever saw in my life. And all right there in a handy carrying case with a handle. All I had to do was take it. Well, the guys were completely wasted, so I took off."

"You left them there?"

The man shrugged. "They would have done the same to me."

Truman sighed. "Fine. So you came into a large sum of money. What did you do with it, as if I couldn't guess?"

"Well, I had nowhere to hide it. I'd been planning to hop a truck and head out of town, but now I had this caseload of money. I didn't want to risk getting caught with it on the bus or get knocked in the head on the road, right? But I couldn't hide it around here, neither."

"Why didn't you put it in the bank?"

"I told you man, I don't have no checking account."

"You could have put it in a safe deposit box."

"Huh?"

"It's a box at the bank. For deposits. In a safe. Hence the name."

"Oh. Well, I didn't know about that."

"And this is when you deposited it into my account?"

"Um, Yeah. I was still carrying around your check, so I just wrote in the account on a deposit slip."

"And why in the world did you do that? I can't imagine you intended for me to enjoy all that money."

"No, man. I just thought I could park it there a few days, and take it back out before you knew anything about it."

Truman shook his head and chuckled. "Really."

Dawkins was offended. "I was desperate, man!

Have you ever had that much money right in your hands?"

"So explain the part where you donated it to charity."

"Yeah, well, after I made that big deposit, I found out that it's way easier to put money in than to take money out. I went back to get a few dollars, right, just a few bucks—and they wouldn't let me have it! Even though I was the guy who made the deposit."

"Funny how that works."

"So since I was already residing here at the shelter, I thought of a way to transfer the money here. So at least it would be closer."

"And how did that work?"

"Well, Bobby at the copy place took the check I had of yours and was able to make some alterations to it. So it looked like you had signed a big check over to the shelter."

"Uh-huh. When I ran into Bobby, I wondered why he gave me the stink eye." Truman sighed. "Okay, so you got hold of some secret money, deposited it all into my checking account, then made a fraudulent check with my signature to transfer all that money over here to the shelter. What did you expect to do then?"

"Well, I thought I could just—I don't know, get it. It was all just slipping through my fingers, and every time I tried something, the money just got farther and farther away. And then the money was here, but I just can't figure out how to get my hands on it. I didn't donate it on purpose."

Truman rolled off his heels and sat down on the cold, hard wooden gym floor. "So these music industry guys—what did they look like?"

Dawkins laughed. "Oh, you do not want to run into these guys! One of them is small and wears a hat—but is he mean! And the other one is like huge. One of the guys here got in his way and the big ape just knocked him down like he was a little dog or something."

THIRTY-SEVEN

Next morning, Truman was driving to beat the band, Geneva in the passenger seat. The Nashville skyline shrinking in the rearview mirror, they were a few minutes from the long highway that pointed them to their destination.

Geneva was only vaguely up to speed. "So, where are we going again?"

Truman kept his eyes on the road. He gripped the wheel so tightly his knuckles were white. "We're going all the way out to Waterdale Homes. There's a studio out that way, and I have reason to believe we'll find Darla Lovell out there."

"The country singer?"

"That's the one."

"But she was kidnapped."

"That was the story. We're heading out to see what's really going on."

"But why would you think the kidnappers are keeping her out there?"

"I was visited by a couple of tough guys—one of whom is rather large and rather violent. These guys apparently work at her record label, and are also somehow involved with this kidnapping business. Dawkins referred to it as a 'publicity stunt'—so we're a little unclear at this point whether the crime is kidnapping or fraud."

"So Mr. Dawkins told you she was out at Waterdale."

"Not exactly—but enough little things add up that I think the place is worth a look. One way or the other, we're going to find out something useful at that house."

"And I had to come with you because..."

"I need you to be a witness."

"A witness?"

"As a good citizen who works for charity — and the daughter of such an influential man. I need someone like you to vouch for me. In case there are any questions."

"But why are we even going out there? Shouldn't we call somebody and report it?"

"Well, the FBI has the point on this case — and the guy in charge has it in him to pin all this on me."

"On you? Why?"

"Well, we have something of a history. So, anyway, I can't risk them getting hold of all the pieces until I know what's what."

"Fine, then what about the police?"

"Same problem. I'm implicated in a federal crime." Truman checked his mirrors and passed another car. "However, I do have a friend on the force — once we find the place, he's the first guy I plan to call."

Geneva began tapping her nails on the dashboard. "This is all a lot to take in. I'm still unclear what this is all about."

"In a nutshell, it's about clearing my name, and it's about determining whether the Fifth Avenue Shelter can keep the money. That's worth a drive out in the country, isn't it?"

"I suppose."

"In the meantime, don't let all this scenery go to waste! Bask in the sunshine streaming through the window. Look at the farmland! Look at the horses! Just because we have serious business doesn't mean we can't enjoy the trip."

"I don't know how you can be so light about this when a girl's life is at stake."

"We don't know that."

"But they said on the news—"

"Take it from me, you can't trust everything you hear from the news. The way I see it, there are a few possibilities here—she might be in on the whole scheme; she was grabbed by someone she knew and trusted, but who betrayed her; or she was snatched by strangers."

"And if she's not in on it?"

"That's why we need to hurry."

They were twenty minutes away from the sub-division.

Fifteen minutes away.

Ten minutes.

Five.

He saw the sign for Waterdale Homes and slowed to make the turn. Inside the sub-division, the car rolled slowly past rows of houses while he squinted at numbers.

Geneva asked, "So you know where we're going?"

"I have a general idea." He saw they were getting near to the house number and pulled to the curb. "We'll walk from here."

"So, are you saying that we'll have to give the donation back?"

He smiled at her. "I guess that depends on whose money it turns out to be."

THIRTY-EIGHT

Truman went to the trunk of the car. He glanced down the block toward the house, and then dug into his identity kit. Coveralls? No. Chaps? No. Jumpsuit?

"What are you looking for?" Geneva was close, too close, her warm breath in his ear.

He shivered and tried to answer. "I'm just," he squeaked, then cleared his throat and tried again. "I'm just looking for a disguise."

"Why are you wasting your time with that? You're not fooling anyone with that stuff."

"Now be fair—I almost fooled you."

"No, you didn't."

"Almost."

She folded her arms. "Whatever."

"Fine." Truman ran his fingers over a few heavy objects sitting loose in the trunk—some wrenches, the jack, a heavy-duty flashlight—and slammed the trunk closed. He looked down at what he was wearing, and unlocked the trunk again. He dug out a wrinkled blazer and slipped it on. He slammed the trunk again. "Okay, let's go."

She gave him the once-over. "That your big disguise?"

"You're not helping." He glanced both ways, then crossed the street and took the sidewalk. As they walked along, he made a futile attempt to smooth out the wrinkles in his jacket.

She asked, "So, what's the plan?"

"Like the man said, I'm making this up as I go." They reached the walkway to the house owned by Unicorn Stinger. He nodded toward it, "There it is."

"Fine." She turned toward it, and he grabbed her

arm.

"Not here. Let's go have a visit with the neighbors."

At the next house, they took the walkway up to the porch. The mailbox had the name Gordon. Truman rang the doorbell.

A couple minutes passed. Geneva let out a sigh. Truman turned and grinned at her.

There was some noise from inside, and then an elderly woman answered the door. "What do you want?"

Truman grinned big teeth. "Hello, ma'am, am I speaking with Ms. Gordon?"

"Mrs."

"Fine, Mrs. Gordon, I'm Bill Taft from The People Who Choose to Vote. We're in the neighborhood today to encourage folks around here to vote their conscience."

The woman narrowed her eyes at him. "You're bothering people and you don't even have a candidate?"

"No, ma'am," Truman replied, wishing he'd thought through his cover story. "We're here to build what they call a grassroots phenomenon. And you, ma'am, strike me as one of the leaders of this community — why, I just bet everyone around here turns to you whenever they need to know what's best for the neighborhood."

"Oh, my word!" The woman blushed and touched the bun on her head to make sure it was in place. "I do suppose that folks around here think of me as a pillar of the community."

"Pillar! That was the word I was looking for." Truman glanced at Geneva for confirmation.

However, Geneva's wide eyes, set jaw, and overall body language indicated that she was not happy with any of this. So he grinned bigger and turned it back on the old woman. "That is why we came to you first. Because we know that you are in a unique position to bring enlightenment to the people in the area around here."

"I'll do what I can."

Truman nodded in the direction of the house next door. "For example, what can you tell me about your neighbors? Doesn't some kind of country music celebrity live over there?"

The woman furrowed her brow. "Actually, there's a studio over there. Folks coming in and out all hours." She leaned forward and added in a low voice, "Who knows what kind of business takes place over there?"

"And what about that young lady—what's her name—Darla Lovell. Have you ever seen her around these parts?"

"I have seen her every so often. She seems like a nice girl. Always waves when I'm in the yard."

"When was the last time you saw her over there?"

"Oh, I suppose just a couple days ago. She came in with those men. I guess they were her bodyguards."

"Could you describe these men?"

"Oh, I don't know that I could. They never really talk with the neighbors. One of them is maybe regular height. And then the other is a giant of some sort. I wonder if that poor boy has a glandular problem?"

"So, did you ever tell anyone about seeing Darla

around here?"

"No. None of my grandchildren really like country music—"

"You didn't call the newspaper?"

"Why would I do that?"

"Well, Darla has been in the news lately. I thought maybe you might have—"

"I don't really watch the news. It's always so depressing! Why, what did the girl do?" The woman leaned forward, her eyes sparkling. "Did she get some drugs or something?"

"Um, no. We won't take up anymore of your time, ma'am. Thank you for your help."

"Oh. Is that it?"

"Yes, ma'am. We've determined that you're exactly the kind of person we need. We'll be in touch."

***

Back on the sidewalk, Geneva asked, "What was all that 'we'll be in touch' stuff? You'll never call her again."

Truman made a face. "I made all of it up—why would you expect that part to be different?"

"It just seems cruel to build up her hopes like that. You don't know how long she'll be looking out the curtains for you to come back."

"I don't think it's all that."

"And did any of that even help?"

"A little. The main thing is that now that we talked to one of the residents along here, it's less suspicious for us to drift over and look in the windows." He walked toward the side windows of the house owned by Unicorn Stinger. "Now we have context."

Geneva followed close behind. She whispered, "I'm a little uncomfortable with all this lying. Is this something you do all the time?"

"It comes with the job."

"I bet there's a more honest way to do it."

"If you don't want to feel like an accomplice, just think of me as the big fat liar, and you're the innocent bystander."

"But I didn't stop you. That's still false witness."

"What are you, a priest?"

"No, but I'm having a long talk with the minister when this is all over."

Truman stood on tiptoes to peek in the side window. Leaning against the warm siding, he peeked through a crack in the curtains. It was a bedroom. The room had an attached bathroom—the light was on in the bathroom. Someone was at the sink, but Truman couldn't see the man's face from this angle—but he did seem to be wearing familiar pin stripes.

Truman headed around back, motioning for Geneva to follow. Across the back of the house, there was a window, the patio doors, and then another window. He peeked in the first window, cupping his hands to shield his eyes from the glare. He saw a kitchen. It was empty.

Gingerly, he inched toward the patio doors. He got on his knees. He peeked—it was a living room. An enormous and familiar man sat on the couch, either moping or napping sitting up. Behind the couch was a door with a padlock on it.

Truman stood. The large man was looking the

other way, so he motioned for Geneva to follow across to the other side. Quickly!

Back pressed against the warm siding, he pushed Geneva back against it, too. When he touched her, he felt a jolt of electricity shoot through him. He shook it off.

At the next window, he saw another bedroom. Nothing to report there.

He and Geneva went around the corner and found another set of three windows. He checked them.

When he was done with all the side windows — he didn't have the nerve to peek in the picture window — he pulled Geneva aside for a conference. "Well, that's that. I don't see her."

"So she's not here."

"Maybe. But there's a padlock on one of the doors in there."

"And what does that mean?"

"People almost never padlock an interior door. Of course, this house is supposed to have some kind of studio — I didn't see any recording equipment, so it might be in the basement. With a lot of expensive equipment like that, I'd certainly put a padlock on the door."

"So it's normal."

Truman took a deep breath and exhaled. "Maybe. But given what we know, that padlock makes me nervous."

"So what do we do now? Now can we call the police?"

"And tell them what? That somebody thought to lock up their valuables? All we have is a lock on the door."

"Huh."

"Besides, if a bunch of flashing lights and sirens come screaming down the road here and surround the house, what happens then? If Darla Lovell is locked up in there, and these guys get desperate, they could do something to hurt her."

"It would only make things worse for them, wouldn't it? It'd be stupid to hurt her."

"Desperate men do stupid things." Truman took a deep breath. He chewed on his lip. He said, "We need to get in there somehow."

Geneva lifted her hands and said, "Lord Jesus, we just implore you—"

"Shhh!" Truman grabbed her wrist and pulled it down. "What are you yelling about?"

"I'm just praying for guidance."

"Aren't I handling it?"

"It looks to me like you need all the help you can get."

"Be that as it may, we're trying to be sneaky here. We don't want to call attention to ourselves. I think even God would understand that."

"I'm not going in there without covering this in prayer."

"Well, could you please pray to yourself?"

"I'm gonna pray for you, that's what I'm gonna do."

"Just quietly. Please."

Geneva turned away, closed her eyes, and started mouthing words. It made Truman nervous, so he looked the other way. He rubbed his eyes and tried to think.

Several seconds passed. He glanced over and whispered impatiently, "Are you done?"

She opened her eyes. "What now?"

"The way I see it, the thing we have to do is to get inside there, somehow get past that goon, and see what's locked up behind that door. For all I know, it's just the closet or the basement. But I have to know before I call in the cavalry."

"So we wait until he leaves?"

"I was thinking more of a distraction. Like if somebody got him to the front door and kept him preoccupied while somebody else went into the house the back way."

"I'm not breaking into any house."

"Actually, I meant that you would be the one who distracts him. You don't even have to tell him any lies—you could make some kind of pitch for the shelter."

"Why me? Why can't you do it?"

"I can't go to the door—these guys know me. They beat me up and everything."

"Really?"

"I'll show you the bruises sometime. So, anyway, there is no way I can be the one at the door. That would not go well. You have to do it."

"But that big guy knows me, too!"

"How does he know you?"

"He was at the shelter with a smaller man. They were hanging around with some of our residents. If I knew they were up to no good, I would have asked them to leave."

"So you talked to them?"

"No."

"Then how do you know he even saw you?"

"How do you know he didn't?"

"So you won't go to the door?"

"No way."

"But if you were to just talk to them about the shelter, how would that—"

"You're better at that kind of thing. Wear one of your fake beards or something."

Truman grimaced. After the incident back at the apartment, he did not want to face that gorilla again. Not alone. And certainly not on the man's own turf.

Geneva asked, "So, what do we do?"

"Well, somebody has to go to that door."

THIRTY-NINE

Sherman Clayton started with the medicine cabinet. Wearing a set of rubber gloves, he emptied the cabinet item by item, tossing each into a little plastic grocery bag. Aspirin, toothpaste, toothbrush, hair tonic, cold medicine, all of it.

All the while thinking of the plan. It was time to cut his losses and get out of town—but that wasn't something he could do lightly. There was some baggage that needed to be dealt with first.

When the plastic bag was full, he tied it off and set it aside. He dumped some powdered cleanser on a damp cloth and wiped each shelf meticulously. Then he moved onto the sink.

Wherever he decided to go, he would certainly be set for a few months while he got settled—this coin he'd grabbed turned out to be worth quite a few bucks. In fact, the guy at the pawnshop offered $20,000 for it. Which, of course, meant it was worth a lot more.

He poured out the cleanser around the sink and then wiped with the wet towel. He was careful to wipe off the faucet, the knobs, and all around the basin. Any surface he might have touched at some point. He moved on to the shower.

How far could somebody get with 20,000 bucks? It was quite a while since he studied the prospect of skipping the country, but he seemed to recall there were no extradition agreements between the U.S. and much of South America.

Or maybe he should go to some island in the Pacific? As he scrubbed the tile, Clayton thought of sandy beaches, palm trees, and bronzed girls in grass skirts. He smiled.

When he was done with the bathroom, he threw all the loose materials in a garbage bag, which he twisted closed. He pulled the door to the bathroom closed behind him.

Out in the bedroom, he began pulling all the bedclothes off the bed—comforter, blankets, sheets, pillowcases. He stuffed them into a fresh plastic bag.

Before he left town, he'd have to do something about the witnesses, of course. Even if his destination was out of the reach of the U.S. government, there were a lot of stops between here and there. He didn't need any loudmouths spouting off before he got away.

First off, he had to kill Darla Lovell. Whether Buddy and Bull Ron could face it or not, that was really the only way to go.

He went to the closet and slid the big mirror door open. He began pulling out his clothes by the hangers, dropping each item into another plastic bag. Shirts. Pants. Ties. Belts.

Of course, before he took care of Darla, he'd have to deal with Bull Ron. The big lug had developed an attachment to the girl—he'd only let something happen to her over his dead body. So, Clayton thought to himself, he might as well just make it official.

Clayton knelt and grabbed each loose pair of shoes, tossing them one at a time into the bag. It pained him, but he needed to travel light. And he couldn't leave any of this stuff behind—who knew how much the cops could get out of this stuff? DNA, clothing tags, whatever. Better to get rid of it than to risk it. When he had emptied the closet, he got the cleanser and wiped it good. He'd worry about the carpet when he was ready to vacuum the whole room.

He moved to the dresser and began pulling out the drawers. He dumped each drawer out on the naked bed.

Of course, he would need to get rid of the boss, too. Buddy Powell had clearly lost control — and he was too powerful, too connected, and, frankly, too scary to be left running around loose. Once Clayton took care of the girl and the bull, who knew how the boss would react? Who he might call? No, better to just cut the snake off at the head and be done with it.

Clayton had filled another garbage bag with all the contents of the drawers. He tied it off. He got the cleanser and wiped down the dresser but good.

He got a fresh bag and moved onto the nightstand. As he emptied the drawers, he wondered about those homeless guys. Whatever happened to them? If he could track them down, he'd take care of those loose ends, too. But as it was, he just had to trust that wherever they were, those two were in no mental state to report anything to the cops.

When Clayton was done with the drawers, he used some cleanser to wipe down the nightstand and the lamp. There, all done.

He put all the garbage bags on top of the bed. He didn't want to take them out through the living room and risk being seen by Bull Ron. He was too busy to come up with any explanations just right now.

He closed the bedroom door behind him and headed for the kitchen. He started with the cabinets, pulling out all the plates and dishes and glasses and coffee mugs. He got them all out on the counter and started fitting them, piece by piece, into the dishwasher. He couldn't remember when or how he might have touched any of these with bare skin, so it was safer to just wash them all over again.

"Whut are you doing?"

Clayton dropped a coffee mug and it shattered on the linoleum floor. He looked at Bull Ron in the doorway and had to count to ten just to make sure he replied in a casual tone of voice. "Just doing some cleaning."

"But those look fine."

"Well, there's a lot of colds going around. Better safe than sorry. You don't want Darla to get sick, right?"

"You dropped something."

"Yeah. Clumsy me. Don't you worry, big fella, I'll clean it up."

The big man stared, slack jawed. His eyes were dull. Finally, he just grunted and wandered off.

Clayton had to sit for a second. He fought to catch his breath, fought the blackness that curled at the edges of his conscious, fought the possibility of his heart exploding in his chest.

When he was relatively calm again, he picked up the fragments of shattered pottery and dropped them in the wastebasket. Then he resumed filling the dishwasher. When it had all the dishes it would take, he pulled open a drawer and started transferring silverware. Forks, knives, spoons, all the utensils that fit.

He had to figure out the best way to deal with the bodies. Could he take them somewhere and dump them? The girl maybe, but no way could he move that Bull Ron anywhere. Not without a forklift.

Once the dishwasher was full, he put in some detergent, set the dials, and started it. He poured out some more cleanser around the sink, dampened a fresh cloth, and wiped good the sink, the faucet, the knobs, the cabinet shelves, and the cabinet doors.

If he just left the girl and Bull Ron in the basement, Clayton wondered how long before the bodies would be found. With Buddy also dead, the soonest anyone would swing by the studio would be when someone came out to deal with Buddy's affairs. How long would that take?

Next, he went to the freezer. He pulled out anything he might have touched or tasted, dropping each frozen brick into the plastic bag. Clayton wondered how hard it would be to dig graves in the basement. The basement had a concrete foundation. Even if he could somehow sneak a jackhammer in past the neighbors, he doubted he could make the rubble not look like fresh graves. Not if he was planning to make a fast exit — the faster, the better.

He wondered about torching the house. That would bring out the fire department, but was it possible to at least burn up the bodies — and evidence — before they got here? No, that seemed too risky.

He opened the door to the refrigerator, and examined the contents. He took all the liquids over to the sink, switched on the cold and hot water, and poured every container out into the drain. Every container of food went into another plastic bag.

He twisted off the bags that were now full, and carried them back into his bedroom. He set them on the bed with the others. He would wait until he killed the girl and Bull Ron, and then he would calmly take each bag out and—what? He couldn't set them on the curb for pickup. And they wouldn't all fit in his car. Maybe he could set them on fire in the basement—was it possible to disable all the smoke and fire alarms?

Oh, well. He'd figure it out when the time came. He reached in his pocket and felt the coin. Like some talisman, it gave him strength.

He closed the door to the bedroom behind him and headed for the living room. He looked at the furniture, the walls, furnishings, and tried to remember what he might have touched and when. He weighed the difficulty of dealing with them against the possibility of them providing evidence against him.

He locked his fingers together and analyzed the room. He stared at the fireplace and wondered how long it would take him to burn all his belongings in there. As he tried to imagine it, he decided that would take way too much time.

He glanced around the room. Wait—what happened to his chess set? His $500, limited edition, numbered Lord of the Rings chess set?

"Bull Ron!" His anger was overriding his common sense. "What have you done with my chess set?"

The big man lumbered in from the other room. "Whut, you mean the checker set?"

"No, I mean the chess set! The one that I paid $500 for! The one that is a numbered limited edition from the Lord of the Rings collection!"

"Downstairs."

"It's—" Clayton bit his lip. He would have to get rid of the set anyway. If it was numbered, that meant there was a sheet somewhere in the world with that number on it. "Fine."

"You want me to get it?"

"In a minute." Clayton turned for the bedroom. He would get his gun, he would tuck it into his pocket, and then he would get the big guy and the girl together in the basement and he'd just pop them both right now. He'd had enough and it was time to go. "Give me a second, and then we can go down and visit Darla together."

"Visit her?"

Clayton went to his room. He yelled, "Yeah, I think it's time to let her go! Don't you?"

"Yeah?"

Clayton grabbed his gun. "Of course! Just give me a second, and then we can—"

He was interrupted by the doorbell.

FORTY

The front door chimed again. Sherman Clayton, who had finally screwed up enough nerve to just shoot his partner and the girl and be done with it, was annoyed by the interruption.

He had no idea who it could be. For all he knew, it was just strangers passing by—maybe door-to-door religious nuts, or just some kid selling candy for a school trip.

His plan was to hold his breath and just wait it out, until whoever it was finally wandered on to their next stop. Then he would lure Bull Ron downstairs and shoot him in the head. And then he'd shoot the girl, and figure out what to do about the bodies. He was still leaning in the direction of—

Wait. What happened to Bull Ron?

With a rush of panic, he realized that the big man had gone to the living room with the intention of opening the door. Clayton checked his gun—yep, still tucked in the back of his pants, hidden by his jacket—and ran for the front to stop the moron.

He was too late. Bull Ron had opened the door and was nonplussed to be faced with a pizza delivery. The big man was scratching his head. "Whut?"

The man at the door—who wore a bizarrely thick and impossibly crooked moustache—checked the paper attached to the square box. "Double pepperoni."

Clayton stopped behind the big guy. He snapped, "You're at the wrong house! We didn't order any pizza."

The pizza guy with the crooked moustache

frowned, glanced to his left, then again at the paper on the box. He read off the address. "Ain't that here?"

Clayton frowned. "Yes, that's the address."

"Then I definitely have a delivery for here. For a—" The guy checked the paper again. "Darla Lovell."

Clayton felt the vein pulsing in his forehead. Did the girl find a phone hooked up downstairs? But if she did, why call for a pizza instead of the cops? He licked his lips and asked nervously, "Was she the one who called it in?"

"I don't know, sir, I don't handle the telephones. I just drive the car. Listen, I need to get my cash and go—I got other deliveries to make, you know?"

Clayton's head trembled in the general direction of up and down. How did this guy know Darla Lovell was here?

"Hey," Bull Ron told the guy, "your face is crooked."

The pizza guy craned his neck up to the one-faced Mt. Rushmore. "Huh?"

"Your face don't match your moustache."

"Oh."

Clayton was too rattled to pay attention to the man somehow straightening his moustache. "Here, I'll just pay you for the stupid pizza."

"No, sir. I have instructions that I can only deliver it personally to Miss—" He checked the sheet again. "Darla Lovell. In person."

"Um." Clayton put a hand to his temple and rubbed. He couldn't take much more of this or the vein would just pop and shoot his blood all over the house. "She's not here, so you'll have to just—"

The big guy bellowed, "Whut's going on? Whut's this all about?"

Clayton and the pizza guy both looked up at the face on the top of the mountain. The giant man was clearly growing confused. Agitated. Clayton knew this was not good.

The pizza guy said, "Look, man, I'm just doing what I was told." He turned to his left and said, "I don't even understand what's going on."

The guy must have had somebody with him. Clayton asked, "Who — ?"

Bull Ron jumped forward, his large frame blocking the sun. Then just as suddenly he was falling backward, a mighty oak falling in the woods.

Clayton had to jump out of the way to avoid the massive body. He looked at the doorway and saw Truman standing there, gripping what looked like the remains of a big metal flashlight. It was damaged by an enormous dent, the face of the flashlight now spilling fragments of the lens and bulb.

Clayton reached around behind him, trying to get beneath the flap of his jacket. Finally, he gripped the gun and whipped it around. "All, right — hold it! Everyone just stop!"

The pizza guy dropped his box and Truman dropped his broken flashlight and both put up their hands. A black woman peeked in from behind Truman, made a face, and also put up her hands.

Clayton said, "Okay, now come in here. Nice and slow."

The pizza guy asked, "Who has to come in?"

"All of you."

The pizza guy said, "Aw, man!"

As the three came in, Clayton wasn't too thrilled

himself. He was *thisclose* to figuring out what to do with two bodies, and now he had to worry about five of them. There was no way he was going to dig five graves in the basement himself.

Truman said, "Come on, let the kid go. You don't need him."

The black woman sassed, "Don't need him? Y'all don't need me, either!"

Clayton sighed. "Nobody is going anywhere!"

Pizza Guy, hands still in the air, shifted his weight from foot to foot. He mumbled to the floor, "Oh, man, oh, man, oh, man."

Truman turned to the woman. "When you pay the kid for the pizza, give him a good tip for wearing the fake moustache. And you should probably throw in a couple bucks hazard pay."

"Oh, man, oh, man, oh, man."

The woman's eyes grew wide. "Me pay him? Why don't you pay him? It was your crazy idea to call him in the first place."

"Well, if you recall, all my money is tied up in your shelter. Or had you forgotten?"

Clayton heard the word "money" and snapped to attention. He pointed the gun at Truman. "That's right, what about the money? I don't suppose you brought it?"

"I already told you. I don't have any of the money. I never did."

"But the FBI said you did."

"It was all a big misunderstanding. Here, let me call them and they can come out and explain it." Truman made a move toward the next room.

"Hold it! What kind of idiot do you think I am?"

"Actually, I'm still working that out."

"Hey!"

"I mean, I'm working out how we can all come to some amicable agreement. Now, if you would just allow us to go on our way, we can get out of your hair—"

"Shut up! Just shut up and let me think!"

Truman, Geneva, and Pizza Guy kept their hands up and their mouths closed while they watched Clayton rubbing his forehead. Truman listened intently to the silence, straining for any clue there was a girl being held hostage somewhere in this house. He gradually became aware of a low droning noise, which gradually turned into a moan.

The beast on the carpet stirred. Everyone turned to watch as he struggled up to a standing position. He still seemed dazed, swirling a bit on his feet. The big man looked at Truman and squinted.

Truman braced himself for a bellow, followed by an attack from a raging locomotive.

But all the beast man said was, "Hey."

Truman smiled uncertainly. "Hey."

"I thought you were the other guy."

"Excuse me? Oh. You mean him?" Truman tilted his head toward Pizza Guy. "It's because he has my moustache."

"Uh."

"Look." Truman reached over and ripped off the man's fake moustache. "See?"

Pizza Guy threw his hands on his face. "Aaaaargh!"

"Oh, don't be such a baby."

"That hurts, man!"

"No," Bull Ron said. "I thought you were the other guy at the place."

Clayton squinted up at the big man. "Bull Ron, what are you talking about?"

"When you sent me back to get the rabbit's foot, I tried to tell him something and then he yelled at me and then I went to hit him and he jumped out the window."

Truman nodded. "Well, I did jump out the window."

"No, I mean the second time."

Geneva asked, "Honey, how many times did you jump out the window?"

"Trust me, one time is enough. Hey, you called me 'Honey.'"

"Don't get used to it."

Truman turned to Clayton. "Look, you and I are men of the world here, right? You don't have to put a gun on us like this. Surely we can talk this out."

Clayton still held the gun on them. His eyes flickered from one person to the next—including Bull Ron. Just in case.

Truman tried again. "Look, you don't want to do anything stupid. The Feds will be here soon enough. And Mrs. Gordon knows we're here."

Clayton squinted. "Who's that?"

"The sweet old lady who lives next door. Don't tell me you don't know your own neighbor?" He clucked his tongue and glanced toward Geneva. "You know, that's the problem with folks today, they just get so busy that they don't take the time to get to know their own neighbors."

Clayton stared at Truman. "Wait a second. If the FBI thinks you have the ransom—then they might just also think you're the kidnapper."

"Like I said, a misunderstanding."

"And if the Feds already think you're the kidnapper, how about if they find you with her?"

Truman exchanged a glance with Geneva. He asked, "So you can take us to her?"

"All y'all head through there. We're going downstairs." Clayton grinned and started motioning with the gun for everybody to move into the next room. "When they find you and Darla together in the basement, they'll have all the proof they need. And I'll be free to go my own way."

Pizza Guy said, "Ohmanohmanohman."

Truman glanced at the big guy, who lumbered along beside the group. The man had to hunch his shoulders to fit through the hallway. Truman thought of the time these boys came after him in his apartment. He remembered the little man telling the big man that Truman was the reason that Darla was in trouble. He remembered how the big man reacted. He said, "Oh."

Clayton's head snapped toward him. "What?"

"Well, I just figured out that the big guy wasn't calling me 'Darling.'"

"Darling? Why would he call you darling?"

"Well, that's what it sounded like at the time. Gimme a break, I was under duress. Anyway, Darla Lovell is not in on the scam, is she? You got her locked up, then?"

"You'll be joining her in a minute. And then when the cops show up, they'll have all the evidence they need that you're the fella who kidnapped her."

Geneva frowned. "But she'll just tell them the difference. Won't she?"

Truman said, "He doesn't plan on Darla telling anyone the difference."

Clayton grinned. "Smart man."

Truman turned to Bull Ron. "You hear that, you big ape? He's going to kill Darla."

Bull Ron's face turned dark. His breathing grew heavier. You could almost see the wheels turning, the smoke coming out of the ears. He slowly turned toward the smaller man.

Clayton, the blood draining from his face, held the gun in his trembling hand. "W-wait a second now. He's just trying to rile you."

The big man took a step toward the little man. The little man took a step back.

Truman turned to Geneva and murmured, "This ought to be good."

"Don't you see?" The wobble in Clayton's gun hand grew worse. "It's the only way! Stay back!"

The bull lunged, meaty paws grabbing for the small man. The small man fired his gun.

BLAM.

BLAM.

And the big man fell on top of him.

Truman grabbed Geneva by the arm. "Take the kid out and call the cops!"

"What about you?"

"I'm getting the girl!" Truman squeezed past the huddle wrestling on the hall floor and found his way to the big den he'd seen through the patio doors. He limped fast as he could to the padlocked door, and yanked uselessly on the lock.

He glanced around for something big to bash it with. His eye caught the tools by the fireplace and he went and got the poker. Rushing back to the padlock, he stuck the poker through the loop in the lock and twisted. No good.

He adjusted the angle of the poker to get the right leverage and tried again. He grunted loudly. Still no good.

He was getting ready for a third try when he glanced over and saw the small end table.

Ah. A key.

He pulled out the poker and dropped it to the carpet with a loud thud and jumped for the key. He fumbled with the key in the lock, and got it open.

He threw wide the door and looked down the stairs into blackness. He felt for a switch and flipped it up and down but nothing changed.

So he carefully took the steps down. His way was lit by the slivers of light coming from the doorway behind him.

He got to the bottom, and stepped on what looked like a little doll. In the dim pool of light he couldn't tell.

He looked around the basement. Outside the dim light from above, all was blackness. He took a measured step. He cleared his throat. "Hello?"

Something walloped him on the back of the head. And then he was out.

FORTY-ONE

Truman was lying on the carpeted basement floor, trying to figure out where he was and how he got here. The carpet felt like sandpaper against his face. The back of his head throbbed.

Slowly, recent events flooded his brain. Of course, none of the memories really explained why he was on the floor here. He remembered walking down into the darkness of the basement, then something clobbering him from behind.

Eventually, he realized there was light. He struggled to turn and squint into the lit room — the room he could see from this vantage point looked like a den. Eventually, he realized that someone was hovering, a female. It was a young lady, probably in her late teens, long blonde hair hanging over her shoulders. Her blouse was wrinkled like she'd been wearing it for days. She was speaking to him in gibberish.

As the cloud in his brain dissolved, he realized the problem was not the speaker, it was the receiver. As he regained his senses, he began to make out what she was saying. Something about being sorry.

He pushed himself up and leaned on one arm. He squinted up at her and croaked, "Darla Lovell, I presume?"

"Yes! Who are you?"

"I'm here to rescue you. I think."

"I'm so sorry that I hit you! I thought you were someone else."

"It's fine. Just the kind of week I'm having." He rubbed that back of his head. "What in the world did you hit me with?"

"The checker board."

"Wow, if you can knock me senseless with a flimsy bit of cardboard—"

"It's made of some kind of rock. Marble maybe."

From the open door at the top of the stairs, the sounds of footsteps floated downward. Truman forced himself to stand, then leaned against the stairs while he got his balance. "I think someone is coming. Is there some back way out of here?"

The girl frowned. "Do you think I'd still be down here if there was another way out?"

"Oh, sorry. Then let's get out of the way until we see who comes down."

Truman set the girl behind the couch to hide. He ran around to the other side of the stairs and stood as far back as he could. Then he realized he needed something for a weapon. He didn't know where this legendary checkerboard was, so he ran over to a microphone stand. He grabbed it, hefted it in his hands to determine whether it worked better as a spear or club, then dragged it over to the stairs back to his hiding place.

He looked at the lights around him and wished he knew where the switch was located. He knew from experience that it was way easier to clobber a guy in the dark if he can't see you coming.

Someone stood in the door at the top of the stairs. The person was breathing heavily. The person took the first step and then paused. Then another step. And another step.

From his hiding place, tucked at the far side of the stairs, Truman gripped the mic stand with both hands. The long metal pipe angled over his shoulder was awkward, and growing heavy.

He saw shoes, then shins, legs, and then the little man with the gun, his jacket torn, blood smeared on his face.

Truman tried to position the awkward metal club but before he could make his swing the little man crouched and pointed the gun right at him. "Put that down."

Truman complied. His arms were relieved, the rest of him less so.

The little man motioned with the gun for Truman to move across to the den. He said, "Glad to find you down here. I wanted to get you and the girl together." The man glanced around. "Darla! Come out here!"

The girl stood and meekly walked around and sat on the couch. She slouched in defeat.

Truman sat next to her. "It won't do you any good," he told the man with the gun. "My friends have already called the cops by now. Not to mention, there's probably some large body on the floor upstairs."

"Ronald!" Darla shot up from the couch. "You killed him!"

Clayton frowned and pointed the gun at Truman. "This man made it necessary. He turned Bull Ron against me. I had no choice."

"I don't believe anything you say."

The man sighed. "Yes, I suppose there's no point lying to you now. The fact is, I did intend to kill him. And now I'm going to kill the both of you."

"Now, wait a second," Truman said, forcing himself to stay seated. No sudden moves. "Let's think this through—why kill us? As it is, your crimes are relatively minor. And you could argue that you killed the big guy in self-defense. He attacked you. You got witnesses. Why add murder on top of that?"

"I think I'll get a lot farther if I just kill you now."

"Ah. I sort of wish you hadn't said that." Truman stood, trying to figure out what else he could say. He was fresh out of words. He looked at Darla. She had tears in her eyes.

There was a racket on the stairs. Either the zoo lost an elephant or Bull Ron had made a comeback and he was coming down.

The little man's face grew white. He turned for the stairs. He went over and looked up. He fired once, twice.

There was the sound of breath escaping a dying animal, and the beast collapsed and tumbled down the stairs. Bull Ron tumbled down and ended at the base of the stairs in a big heap. Incredibly, he was still breathing.

Clayton turned to his captives and the last thing he saw was Truman's fist.

FORTY-TWO

Marion Russell was working in the garden. How long had he been here at the sanctuary — two days? three? He had completely lost track of time.

When Mr. Stone had brought him out here, Marion was anxious, fearful, and desperate. All the negative feelings that had flowed through him were dragging him down to the earth.

But in his short time here with the brethren, Marion found his soul was so much lighter now. They had trusted him enough to give him a shift working in the garden. He wore a hooded brown robe, crawling through the rows of vegetables on his hands and knees. As he yanked out the weeds, he found that the workout served as an amazing stress reliever. He had never felt this much at peace. He couldn't remember the last time he sneezed.

He closed his eyes and smiled. He imagined that all his stress was leaving him like helium leaking from a balloon. That was an exercise one of the brothers taught him after meditation.

Marion found that he had achieved an emotional distance from all the things and all the people that had pressed in on him: His boss at the Internal Revenue Service. Mr. Mittens' ranking in the World Dog League. His wife, Shirley. That man Truman. His former life of crime.

He felt no anxiety. He felt no hatred. All he felt was love.

Marion serenely dug his hands into the loose earth and pulled some more weeds. He found himself wondering the best way to send for his wife and his dog. How to explain the new life that he found. How to explain the joy that awaited them here. How to explain he'd signed over the deed to the house so they had to move somewhere anyway.

A twinge of anxiety passed through him. He had been enjoying his solitude. But if Shirley and Mr. Mittens were to join him here…

Marion closed his eyes, and breathed deeply. In and out. In and out. Helium out of a balloon. Helium out of a balloon.

"Brother Marion."

Marion squinted up at another man in a hooded robe. The man stood directly between Marion and the sun, a halo around him. "Yes, Brother Franklin?"

"We were wondering whether you were up for a shift guarding…*her.*"

Marion felt a shock of elation jolt through him. He pushed off the ground and jumped to his feet, wiping the loose dirt off his hands. "You mean…" He leaned forward and whispered the rest. "…the *sacred relic?*"

The other man, his hands hidden in the sleeves of his robe, nodded. "That is correct, Brother Marion. This is a very special opportunity we are affording you. But you have come along quite well in your short time here. Few have given so much to the order so quickly."

"It has been my honor."

"We are the ones who have been honored. And the elders feel that perhaps you are ready to join us in the inner circle."

"When do I start?"

"Come with me." The man turned and led Marion out of the garden and back toward the lodge. It was an enormous house deep in the woods, far away from the nearest public road.

They reached a big double door to the cellar. The other man, hands still in his sleeves, stepped back and waited for Marion to pull them open. Then he led the way down the steps.

The walls of the cellar were stone. It was cool down there. It was also dim, only lit by a single bulb hanging from the low ceiling.

The man led Marion over to the far wall, where another man in a hooded robe stood watch over a small door. Brother Franklin said, "You are relieved, Brother Thomas. Brother Marion here is now being welcomed to the inner circle."

Brother Thomas nodded without speaking and walked away. He went to the stairs leading into the house and ascended.

Marion looked expectantly at Brother Franklin, the excitement building inside him. How should he conduct himself in such a moment? Was he allowed to ask questions? Should he keep his silence? What did the elders expect of him?

"I suppose you have many questions, Brother Marion."

"I am here to serve."

"Then come and see." Brother Franklin reached for the handle and pulled open the door. He led Marion into a smaller inner room and yanked the chain on the single bulb hanging from the ceiling.

In the dim light, Marion saw four plain wooden benches set around a wooden pedestal. A podium. Or, perhaps, an altar.

On top of the pedestal was a squiggly object. Marion stepped forward. He leaned over it. It was...

It was ...

"What is it?"

"This is the sacred relic."

"Yes, but what is it?"

"Lo, these many years it has been hidden from the eyes of the commoners. It has held this hallowed place of honor among those of us who understand."

"Yes," Marion answered patiently. "But what is it?"

"The vulgar have referred to it as the 'Nun Bun.'"

Marion looked at it. He had heard of this object—a cinnamon roll that had, miraculously, taken on the visage of Mother Theresa. For a time, it had been on display at a Nashville-area coffeehouse. And then it was stolen and never seen again.

And now it turned out that it was here. Where monks guarded it around the clock.

Brother Franklin said, "Now you are truly one of us."

Marion sneezed. "I gave away my house for this?"

FORTY-THREE

Lt. Detective Wagner was driving out to Waterdale Homes with all haste. When the news came across his desk that somebody was believed to have found Darla Lovell—and Truman was somehow involved after all—Wagner knew he needed to get out there and see what was what.

Of course, the whole drive out there he was trying to think of ways to not have the man stay with him. Friends were friends, but Truman was a pig. Wagner wished his wife would get back from her mother's.

He saw the sign for Waterdale and made the turn. He squinted at the numbers on mailboxes and front doors. Knuckles white on the steering wheel, hunched over, he slowly navigated his way through the subdivision.

He looked ahead and guessed he'd found the place. Of course, all the emergency vehicles made it easy—in front of the house were an ambulance, a fire truck, a couple police cars, and even a few vans from the local TV news.

Wagner pulled his car along the curb and parked. With all the vehicles in the yard and along the road, he was a good half-block away. He was hoofing it toward the house in question when he saw an older woman, apparently the next-door neighbor, standing in her front yard, craning her neck toward the house as if the action somehow gave her x-ray vision. She noticed Wagner and waved to him. "Excuse me, are you involved?"

Wagner stopped. "'Involved'?"

"You know," the woman said, inching closer.

She asked in a low voice, "Are you one of them?"

"One of whom, ma'am?"

"That political group."

"Um, no." Wagner made a face. "What political group?"

"All I know is that a gentleman and a young lady came to my door asking questions about these people here, and now there are all these emergency vehicles. I didn't know if maybe this was all, you know…" She leaned even closer. "…*politically* motivated."

"I wouldn't know."

She wrapped her arms around herself like she was cold. "I know that politics have gotten ugly, but this seems rather sort of extreme, don't you think?"

Wagner shook his head. "Actually, I'm here to find out what's what."

At the door, locals and members of the local media were straining to see past the uniformed officer standing guard. Wagner walked up to the officer and flashed his badge. "Who's in charge of the scene?"

"Lt. Drake. You'll find him inside, sir."

"Thanks." Wagner made to enter when the door was suddenly blocked: Paramedics were dragging out a gurney, stretched to the max, carrying an enormous man who barely fit. The enormous man was pale and still, but he wore an oxygen mask instead of a sheet, so he must have had a fighting chance.

Wagner stepped out of the way. The uniformed officer held out his arms to figuratively push the crowd back to make room for the paramedics and their patient.

Inside, the front room was empty. He heard voices from down the hall.

He knocked on a closed door and peeked in. It was a bedroom, the bed stripped of its bedclothes— yet, strangely, topped with a pile of garbage bags. A little man in a striped suit sat on the edge of the bed, while two uniformed officers spoke with him. They stopped and turned to the intruder.

Wagner asked, "Lt. Drake?"

The officers shook their heads. One pointed to his left. "Back that way."

"Thanks."

In the den, a young blonde girl sat in a big recliner. He thought he recognized her as Darla Lovell. An EMT was attending to her.

He looked in another door and found a set of stairs. Voices were floating up from down there. He went down to the basement, stepping over a few brown spots that he suspected were blood.

He found Truman sitting on a couch, next to a stunning woman. A man in a rumpled suit paced and asked questions.

Truman did not appear distressed. In fact, he waved and said, "Hiya, Mike!"

The man in the rumpled suit whirled to see the newcomer. "And who's this?"

Wagner flashed his badge. "Lt. Mike Wagner. Are you Lt. Drake?"

"Ayup. To what do we owe the pleasure?"

"I just came by to see how things were going. Is Truman here in any trouble?"

"What? No. Should he be?"

"I'm asking you."

Drake yawned and stretched his back. "Not so

far as I can tell. But we'll have a few folks rounded up by days end."

"Is it all right if I sit in here?"

"Actually, we're about done. I'll go check on my boys upstairs, if you'd like to have a few words."

As Drake shambled up the steps, Wagner asked, "So, Truman, what did you get yourself into now?"

"I promise, Mike, I intended to call you. But then things got a little out of hand here. You know how these wild parties get."

"Yeah." Wagner's eyes flickered to the woman. "Are you going to introduce me?"

"Oh, I'm sorry — this is Geneva Phillips. Geneva, this is my friend on the force, Lt. Detective Mike Wagner."

Geneva stood and held out a hand. "Pleased to meet you."

"The pleasure is mine." Wagner took the smooth hand and shook it lightly. He had to remind himself to let go. He looked at Truman. "So, who all is he rounding up? And is that, in fact, Darla Lovell upstairs?"

"Let's see, to answer your questions in order: The people who either have or will soon have warrants for their arrest are Buddy Powell, Wanda Lovell — that's the mother of Darla, poor kid — and that weasel upstairs in the striped suit, Sherman Clayton. On charges of, let's see, insurance fraud, kidnapping, false imprisonment, assault, and corrupting a minor. And, I'm sure, some more charges by the time it's done."

"Uh-huh."

"And yes, that is Darla Lovell upstairs. Country music star and kidnapping victim. It's a sad story when you hear it out."

"Are you writing it?"

"Who me? I don't have the column anymore."

"Uh-huh. And who was the big guy on the stretcher?"

"That would be Bull Ron, the beast that walks like a man. He was in on the kidnapping, but in the end he got shot trying to protect the girl. I get the feeling he was duped into helping, so the courts should go easy on him."

Wagner looked at Geneva. "I'm sorry, and how do you fit into all this?"

Truman spoke up, "She works at the charity where all the ransom money went."

"I'm the manager at the Fifth Avenue Shelter." Geneva frowned. "I guess we'll have to return all the money now."

"Afraid so, darling," Truman nodded. "It belongs to the insurance company."

Wagner said, "By the way, I saw a friend of yours earlier."

"Really? Who?"

"Jack Carlin."

"Where? Out at the lake?"

"Hospital."

"Working a story?"

"I don't think he'll be working any stories anytime soon. Apparently, he jumped from your apartment window and broke several bones."

Truman and Geneva looked at each other and laughed.

"That's funny?"

Truman wiped an eye with his sleeve. "I guess you had to be there."

A commotion could be heard at the top of the stairs. Wagner went up, followed by Truman and Geneva.

In the den, two men in black overcoats had interrupted the doctor's exam of the young lady. One of them was demanding of the doctor, "Who is the officer in charge?"

Truman peeked over Wagner's shoulder. "Hey! How's tricks?"

Special Agent Charles "Bow-Wow" Murphy turned red and jabbed a finger in the direction of Truman. "You!" Murphy whirled this way and that, not caring who was actually listening as he pointed again. "Arrest that man!"

Wagner stepped up. "On what charge?"

Murphy snapped, "He's a kidnapper!"

Darla shot up from her chair. "He is not! He's the one who saved me!"

Murphy was taken aback. He regrouped, and pointed again. "Well, then, he is in illegal possession of the ransom money!"

Geneva jumped out from behind the other men. "No, he isn't! The money is at the Fifth Avenue Shelter."

"How would you know that?"

Truman asked, "Guess where she works?"

Murphy was taken aback again. He sputtered, but no more words came out for a bit. Finally, he said weakly, "Destruction of private property?"

Special Agent Reed stepped close and murmured, "Actually, that was us."

Murphy cleared his throat and looked at Truman. "Well, you'll still have to come in for questioning as a material witness."

"I don't think so," Wagner said.

"And who are you?"

Wagner flashed his badge. "Lt. Detective Mike Wagner. This man just aided the police in apprehending a major kidnapping ring. And right now, he is in my protective custody."

"W-wagner?" Murphy stepped back. "Then y-you're the man who stole my witness!"

Wagner squinted. "Who are you?"

Truman leaned in and murmured into his ear, "That's Bow-Wow."

Wagner laughed. "This is 'Bow-Wow'?"

Murphy snapped, "Don't call me that!" He seemed to swoon, and then collapsed into a chair. He mumbled, "It's a conspiracy," followed by a series of mumbles that no one else could make out. Apparently, he wasn't speaking to any of them.

Special Agent Reed said, "Well, it sounds like you have it all in hand." He took Murphy by the arm and said gently, "You know, maybe you should take some time off. It would do you a world of good." He helped Murphy up and began leading him out. He turned back to say, "We'll just get out of your way."

A uniformed officer entered. "Excuse me, folks, we're about to take Mr. Clayton out, but he claims he lost some kind of valuable jewelry or something? Did you see it anywhere?"

Truman and Geneva exchanged a glance and shrugged. Truman said, "He was all over the house. If you look in one of the bedrooms, he was throwing out a bunch of stuff. He had all these trash bags —"

"I saw them, yes."

"Oh. And then he also wrestled with the big guy in the hall. So maybe he could have dropped it there.

Or on the stairs. We were all running around at the end there, so he could have dropped it pretty much anywhere."

Darla shook her head. "I didn't see him drop anything. But I was downstairs the whole time."

Truman added, "When he was unconscious, I frisked him for weapons. But I didn't see any kind of jewelry."

The officer smiled. "Well, thanks anyway, folks." He trotted off.

The doctor had packed up his bag. "Well, young lady, we should go in now for a few tests." He turned to the others. "But she seems like she'll be fine. She just needs a lot of rest."

Darla hugged Truman. "Thank you!"

"Anytime." Truman blushed. When the hug ended, he asked, "So what happens to you now?"

The girl pushed strands of blonde hair behind her ear. "I don't rightly know. I guess I'm all alone."

Geneva said, "I know you don't know me, but if you need to talk or anything, I'm willing to listen. If you want, I can come in with you to the hospital."

"I'd like that. Thank you."

Geneva looked at Truman. "So, what are you doing now?"

"Well, I have a novel to finish."

Wagner said, "With Carlin out of commission for a while, I bet you could get your old column back."

"Crawl back to that place? Please."

Geneva said, "Well, what do you say to dinner some night this week? I'll even buy. I feel like a hero deserves that much."

"Oh, I could never allow a woman to buy my

dinner. I'm too old fashioned for that."

"A women has a right to buy a man dinner."

Truman reached in his pocket and pulled out his new coin. "I'll flip you for it."

The "Nun Bun" was stolen from Bongo Java coffeehouse in Nashville on Christmas Day 2005. Its whereabouts are still unknown. A $5,000 reward is being offered for any information that may lead to the return of the Nun Bun and the successful prosecution of the thieves.

BongoJava.com

ABOUT THE AUTHOR

When he was in the first grade, Chris Well's career plans included growing up to be Batman. The same year that he found out that "Batman" was not actually an occupation, he also began writing made-up stories. Today, he is a novelist and an award-winning magazine editor. He and his wife live in Tennessee. Visit him online at StudioWell.com.

Made in the USA
Las Vegas, NV
20 December 2022

63763424R00177